Middle Aged Love Stories

Josephine Daskam

Middle Aged Love Stories

By

Josephine (Daskam) Bacon

Short Story Index Reprint Series

BOOKS FOR LIBRARIES PRESS
FREEPORT, NEW YORK

First Published 1903
Reprinted 1971

INTERNATIONAL STANDARD BOOK NUMBER:
0-8369-3285-4

LIBRARY OF CONGRESS CATALOG CARD NUMBER:
74-169538

PRINTED IN THE UNITED STATES OF AMERICA
BY
NEW WORLD BOOK MANUFACTURING CO., INC.
HALLANDALE, FLORIDA 33009

TO R. K. C.

WITH MUCH LOVE

CONTENTS

IN THE VALLEY OF THE SHADOW

IN THE VALLEY OF THE SHADOW

TO Belden, pacing the library dog-gedly, the waiting seemed interminable, the strain unnecessarily prolonged. A half-hour ago quick feet had echoed through the upper halls, windows had opened, doors all but slammed, vague whisperings and drawn breaths had hovered impalpably about the whole place; but now all was utterly quiet. His own regular footfall alone disturbed the unnatural stillness of a large house.

Outside, the delicious October sun poured down through an atmosphere of faultless blue. The foliage was thick yet, and the red-and-yellow leaves danced heartlessly in the wind. A year ago they had gone on a nutting-party, and Clarice had raced with the children and picked up more than anybody else. Now — even to think of her brought that faint odor of salts-of-lavender and beef-tea that disheartened him so, somehow, when he sat by her bed coaxing her into sipping the stuff.

Some one was coming down the stairs. It was Peter's step — his new one since last Friday, when they had all, it seemed, begun to walk and talk and breathe a little differently. Belden hurried across the room and caught him at the foot of the steps.

"Well, old man, how goes it?" he demanded, with a determined cheerfulness.

His brother-in-law stared at him emptily.

"It's to-morrow," he said, gripping the newel-post, "to-morrow afternoon. Jameson is coming — they'll do it here. Jame-

son brings his special nurse for the —
the operation, but the other one is due at
five, and you get her just the same. I
told Henry to put up the dog-cart. I
don't know, though — maybe the run-
about — no, the tire's loose. Still, it
might do —"

"For heaven's sake, Peter, don't
bother about it ! I'll find a rig. What
else does he say ? "

"He says there's a good fighting
chance — a very good one. He says her
grit alone — Oh, Belden, what shall we
do? *What* shall we do ? "

Peter sat down heavily on the lowest
stair.

"Only last week she was so well —
and yet she really wasn't. I suppose he
knows. But it doesn't seem possible —
I can't get it through my head. Poor
little Caddy ! She never had a sick day
in her life. No headaches, like most
women, even — no nonsense — Oh, Belden, *what* shall we do ? "

"Brace up, Peter; think what a good fighting chance means, think of that! It's not as if Caddy were old; she has that on her side. She's seven years behind me, you know."

Peter scowled. "You're fifty, aren't you?"

"Not a bit. Only forty-eight, and just that, too. Now you go out and get the nurse, and I'll stay here. It'll do you a lot of good. Don't mope around in the house all day — what's the use?"

"I can't leave the house. Honestly, Belden, I can't. I've tried twice, and I just walk right back. It's no good. There's the cart — and you won't be long, will you?"

Belden took up the reins with a vague sense of momentary relief: it was something to do. Under the influence of the fresh autumn air his spirits rose; he found himself enjoying the swift rattle of the cart and the beat of the horse's feet. After all, think of Caddy's grit; think of her fine constitution! A fighting chance — that was little enough to say, though. Why couldn't he have put it a little stronger? Hitchcock always was a pessimist.

At the station the usual crowd of well-dressed suburbanites quieted their horses and waited impatiently for the express. As Belden drew up into line, they greeted him with a subdued interest; coachmen left their seats to ask how Mrs. Moore was to-day, and when could one see her? A sudden mist came over his eyes as he answered briefly, "Very soon — I hope."

The train thundered in; in an incredibly short time all the guests and commuters were hurried off toward town — where was that nurse?

As his glance wandered through the thinning crowd, it was met suddenly and squarely by two brown eyes set in a fresh pink face framed by dark hair lightly sprinkled with gray. The second that he looked into that woman's eyes taught him her character, absolutely, as finally as if he had grown up with her.   One could trust her to the last ditch, he thought.

She walked straight up to the cart. " I am the nurse sent for by Dr. Hitch-cock.   Are you Mr. Moore? "

" I am Mrs. Moore's brother — Mr. Belden," he explained.   " Have you your checks ? "

" That is all arranged," she returned briefly.   " I am all ready.   May I ask you to hurry ?   Dr. Hitchcock was anx-ious for me to see her before six, when the fever begins."

His nerves were more sharply edged than he knew : an instant irritation seized him.

" There is plenty of room in the back of the cart," he insisted, " the express people are very uncertain.   Would you not better give me the checks ? "

She swung herself up beside him with a firm, assured motion ; for a heavily built woman she carried herself very lightly.

"I think not," she said decidedly, "the man has started, I am sure. I would rather lose no time."

He bowed and started the horse: he disliked her already. To a deep-seated, involuntary disgust that any woman should have to earn her living he added a displeased wonder that one should choose this method of doing it. There must be disagreeable details connected with it, embarrassments, absolute indignities: why did they not marry? This woman was good-looking enough. She was very obstinate — almost dictatorial. His idea of womanhood was hopelessly confused with clouds of white tulle, appealing eyes, and a desire for guidance. It was impossible to connect any of these characteristics with the woman beside him.

For a while they drove in silence. Then compunction seized him and he remarked on the beauty of the foliage. She assented easily, but seemed no more relieved by the speech than embarrassed by the silence. It was impossible to treat her as a hired servant: one felt a strong personality in her. Before they reached the house he was searching for conversation that should not bore her.

As they stepped into the wide hall, where he observed with a shade of displeasure that her luggage had come before them, Dr. Hitchcock met them.

"Ah, Miss Strong, glad to see you. Come right up. On time, as usual, of course! I was afraid you couldn't make it. Jameson comes to-morrow, you know——"

They were up the stairs; Belden stood idly in the hall where they had left him. He had had an idea of showing her the house, stating some of the facts of Clarice's sudden and terrible need of her, indicating that in a family so jarred from the very foundations it would be wiser to look to him than to the bewildered master of the establishment; but this was not necessary.

Evidently she persisted in dispensing with his services.

His hand slipped to his vest pocket, but he replaced the cigar uncertainly: it seemed not quite the thing to smoke. Ought he to go to Peter? In his mind's eye he saw the poor fellow haunting the landing by Caddy's door; he had an idea that in some way he kept things quiet by doing this. And how could one be sure that the troubled creature wanted company?

There was a violent ring at the bell, a jarring of wheels on the asphalt. The door flew open and the prettiest little woman imaginable, all fluffy ends and scarlet flowers and orris scent, rushed toward him.

"Oh, Will! Oh, Will!" she gasped, "isn't it terrible? Where is Peter? Can I see her? Oh, Will!"

Instinctively he took her in his arms — one always did that with Peter's sister — and she put her head on his shoulder and cried a little, while he patted her and murmured, " There, there! "

She was so manifestly comforted, and it was so pleasant to comfort her — this was what a woman should be. He felt a renewed sense of capacity, of readiness for even the most terrible emergency. He led her gently to the great cushioned window-seat and listened sympathetically to her excited babblings.

" It will kill Peter — it will kill him! In — in a great m-many ways, you know, Will, Peter isn't so — so c-calm as Caddy. He is just bound up in her. Suppose — Oh, Will!"

"Don't cry, Sue dear, don't!" he said soothingly. "She has a good chance—a fine chance, really. These things are mostly resisting power, you know, and grit, and think what a lot of grit Caddy's got!"

"Oh, I know, I know! Don't you know when the baby died — that first baby — and s-she was so weak she could hardly speak? 'Never mind, P-Peter, we'll have another!' Oh, dear, she was so pl-plucky, Will! And now to think—"

He choked a little. "I know, I know," he murmured, "Caddy's a brick. She always was."

She sat up, not wholly withdrawing from his arm, and patted her eyes, breathing brokenly. Little gusts of orris floated toward him.

"Where are the children?" she asked, almost herself now.

"They're here—Peter wants them one minute and sends them away the next. I should send them to grandmother's, but he won't hear of it."

A light step sounded on the stair. The nurse appeared on the lower landing. She was dressed in cool blue gingham; the straps of her white apron marked the firm, broad lines of her bust and shoulder.

"Is this Mrs. Wylie?" she said in

her clear, assured voice. "Mrs. Moore would like to see her a moment. Will you come with me?"

"I will come directly," and Sue gathered together her gloves and hand-bag.

"She's very good-looking—it's a pity her hair is so gray," she breathed in his ear. As the two women stood together a moment on the landing he realized, not for the first time, that Sue was a little too small. But he had never thought her sallow before.

Peter came in by the greenhouse door, walking slowly, his hands behind his back. He looked old for the first time in his jolly, persistently boyish life.

"Those chrysanthemums are all drying up," he complained fretfully; "not one of the blamed servants has done a thing since — since — O Lord, Will, what shall we be doing this time to-morrow? Where are the children? Where's Miss Strong? There's a woman for you! Caddy took to her directly. She's there now. She's talking to her about the children. Oh, my God!"

Belden grasped his hand and they walked silently up and down the hall.

"Aunt Lucia's coming to-night," Peter resumed nervously. "She will drive me mad. Take care of her, will you? If I could have choked her off—but when you think she was just like a mother to Cad all these years, what can you do? She's got a right. You'd think she'd have got some sense from living with Cad so long. I told Henry to go for her—and there you are," he added, as the cart drew up before the open door.

Belden went slowly down the steps; he detested Aunt Lucia, and Clarice had always stood between them.

"How do you do?" he began, assisting her from the high seat. Her long crape veil caught in the wheel, and the numberless black and floating ends of her costume wound themselves about him as he bent down to disentangle her.

"Oh, Wilmot, this is a terrible day for us all, is it not? Be careful of the hem of that veil, please. When I kissed Clarice good-by last Christmas I little thought *what* a good-by it was! Is she conscious? You have muddied the boa, I think, but never mind. Can I see her once more?"

"For Heaven's sake, Aunt Lucia, anybody would think Caddy was in her grave! She's a long way from it yet, thank God! Of course she's conscious, and spunky as the — as ever. I don't think you really needed to —"

"My dear Wilmot, I prepared Clarice for her confirmation, I dressed her for her wedding, and I was here when the children were born. If you think that I would fail her in this crisis you have a very poor idea of my character. But then, I am perfectly aware that you always had. Oh, there is Peter! My

[16]

poor Peter!" She rushed toward him, and Belden smiled sardonically as his brother-in-law planted a perfunctory kiss on her chin.

"This may comfort you, Peter, as it has me so often in such circumstances. So short, so true, so helpful. *'Underneath are the everlasting arms!'* Do you feel that, Peter?"

"I — I — yes, indeed, Aunt Lucia — you must want a bite of something, I'm sure, driving so far."

Peter writhed miserably in Aunt Lucia's crape-and-jet arms.

"Not till I have seen her, Peter. Afterwards I shouldn't mind. I have brought such a beautiful address by Bishop Hunter. It was delivered on the occasion of the death of Governor ——, unless I forgot to put it in with my knitted shawl. I believe I did. I will send for it directly. When my dear husband — he was so fond of Clarice — died, I read it more than anything else, except the Prayer-book, of course. You will surely find it a help."

"Yes, Aunt Lucia. Your room is ready, and —"

"Not till I have seen her, Peter."

"Susy is there now, and Miss Strong says nobody else this evening. To-morrow —"

Aunt Lucia drew away.

"Do I understand that Susy Wylie — no relation at all — is preferred before the only mother Clarice has had for all these years?"

Peter winced. "But you weren't here, Aunt Lucia," he argued wearily.

"Who is Miss Strong?"

"Here she is!" There was great relief in Peter's voice. "Miss Strong, my aunt, Mrs. Wetherly."

"Mrs. Moore sends you her best love, and wants you to get thoroughly rested, so that you can see her the first thing in the morning, Mrs. Wetherly. She says you are not to let them frighten you."

As if by magic the formidable frown faded from Aunt Lucia's forehead. She smiled approvingly at the nurse.

"Very well. I should like to ask you a few questions — Clarice was always thoughtful."

They moved away together. The two men stared at each other.

"How do you account for that?" Belden queried.

"Oh, it's her calm way and her voice. You want to do everything she says. Norah says she's sure Mrs. Moore will get well now, with her to take care of her. By George, Will, if she pulls Caddy through it'll be worth her while, I tell you."

"Oh, they always do their best. And they all have that habit, I fancy. It's part of the training."

Peter looked up surprised.

"You don't like her, eh?"

"How absurd. I never considered her particularly. I don't care for masculine, dictatorial women, on general principles — ”

“ Oh, nonsense ! I tell you you’ve taken a grudge against her, and you want to get rid of it as soon as possible.”

“ I suppose I have a right to my opinion,” Belden began hotly, but a wave of remorse surged over him at sight of the other man’s drawn, nervous face.

“ Any one would think we had nothing to do but scrap over a trained nurse,” he said lightly. “ She’s all you say, I haven’t a doubt, old man, and if she pulls Caddy through, I’ll sing her praises louder than any of you.”

They sat in silence. A burst of laughter from the kitchen-garden startled them, and Belden started up as if to check it.

“ Don’t stop ’em — it’s the servants. Why shouldn’t they laugh ? ” said Peter quietly. “ I’ve been thinking it all over. If Caddy — if — if she doesn’t get well, she doesn’t want a lot of black and all that. It's bad for the children. And she said the children oughtn't to grow up without a mother—think of that!"

"I guess that's all right," said Belden sadly. "Look at my boy there!"

A slender, stoop-shouldered lad slouched by the long hall-window, his hands in his pockets, an unlighted cigarette in his mouth.

"Well, well, we all have our load!" Peter's mood had changed utterly, to the other's astonishment. He seemed gentler, more thoughtful, controlled beyond belief.

"I don't see why we shouldn't smoke," he added, and they lighted cigars.

"You see, we talked it all over," he said, half to himself, "and she's so reasonable and calm, herself. . . . She says Margaret's going to grow up just like her. That's a comfort. And there's the boy."

Suddenly the cigar dropped from his lips to the floor.

"Good God, Belden!" he shouted, "I kept thinking she'd be here, too! I forgot — I — Oh, what rot! Do you think I'll stand it? Do you think I'll put up with it? Why didn't Hitchcock know before? It was his business to know! I tell you I'll ruin that man if it takes every dollar I've got!"

Belden stared at him helplessly. Was this Peter, this red-faced, scowling menace? As he watched him silently the nurse came in from the greenhouse.

"Mrs. Moore wants to say good night to you, Mr. Moore," she said, her deep, clear voice echoing strangely after the hoarse passion of Peter's rage. "I found these all picked — were you going to take them to her?"

Peter drew a deep breath and put out a shaking hand for the flowers.

"I don't know what's the matter with me, Will — I talk like a fool," he half whispered. "I can't get used to this damned see-saw. First I'm all ready for it, and

then I'm nearly wild. And so it goes—
up and down, up and down."

"How is she? Is it all settled for
to-morrow? Hitchcock said that perhaps—"

"Mrs. Moore is doing very well—
really very well. She was a little excited
when Mrs. Wylie was with her, but she
is nicely sleepy now. I think it will be
better to stay only a moment. She will
get a good night's rest to-night, it is so
cool. The weather is on our side."

She smiled into his eyes and nodded
gravely. He brightened and squared
his shoulders. As he went quickly up
the stairs, Belden stopped the woman.

"Tell me," he said authoritatively,
"how is my sister, really? What do
you consider her chance?"

She looked him easily in the eyes.
"It is impossible to say," she returned
gravely. "Your sister is a very brave,
self-possessed woman, and seems to have
a good constitution. That is, of course,

half the battle. But her case is very complicated, and until the operation, no one can tell. You may have every confidence in Dr. Jameson. He is a magnificent surgeon."

Before her non-committal eyes his own fell baffled. He was more irritated than he cared to own. Could she not see that he was prepared for anything, that his self-control was as great as her own? She treated him like a child; those professional reserves, necessary, doubtless, in the case of Peter and his excitable sister, were wasted on him. Why could she not see it?

" I am quite aware of Dr. Jameson's skill," he said coldly, " but I had hoped that you would find yourself able to break through the professional attitude sufficiently to give me your real opinion, which, of course, you must have formed."

She threw him a quick glance. " Ah, my friend," he thought exultingly, " you have a temper, then ! " But in an instant it was gone.

" I have told you all I was able to tell," she said evenly. " I have been here but a short time, you know."

She turned and left the hall, and he, chafing under a sense of merited rebuke, conscious of a foolish petulance, went discontentedly into the library. He seemed to be continually at fault with Miss Strong, but unable to resist the effort to master her.

The evening was very lonely and still. Peter had gone to his room early, and the children had effaced themselves: Susy was with them. Aunt Lucia read the " Imitation of Christ," by the fire. Belden's mind turned unconsciously to the old days when Caddy and he dreamed out their future in the nursery. It had all come out just as she had planned, except this. Poor little Caddy — a fighting chance !

The next morning seemed to fly by them : it was nine o'clock, ten, eleven.

At this hour a feverish activity suddenly spread through the house. They met and passed each other, hurrying, troubled, secretive; the servants stumbled and quarrelled in their purposeless haste. To Belden, quieting when he could, sternly optimistic everywhere, at heart heavy and uncertain, it seemed that the one anchor of their hopes was this calm, clear-eyed woman in her uniform of authority!

Peter hung pathetically on her lightest word; the children, dazed and terrified, ate and exercised at her command; his own boy, a strange hard look in his furtive eyes, followed her like a dog, and Aunt Lucia submitted with unprecedented meekness to an abrupt curtailment of her interview with Clarice. He himself went into the bedroom for a moment, half uncertain of the reality of the experience. It was absurd to remember that he might never see her, conscious, again — his own little Caddy.

He sat awkwardly on the side of the bed.

"Well, little woman, how goes it?"

"Queen's taste, Will!"

"Good for you! I'm proud of the Beldens, Caddy — Billy acts like a drum-major."

Her eyes softened.

"The dear boy," she murmured. Their eyes met. "*Look after him*," hers said, and his, "*As long as I live!*" He stooped and kissed her lightly. "Mind you look as well as this to-morrow!"

"Oh, I shall be all right. Miss Strong will take care of me. When I think how I have the best of everything — such care — I've been a very happy woman, Will dear."

His eyes filled. He threw her a kiss and went out blindly.

A hand touched his arm. "You've done her good," said the nurse softly. "You stayed just long enough. She'll take her nap now."

He went heavily into his own room. Below him a little porch led out from the smoking-room, and as he sat lost in a miserable reverie, voices rose from it to his window.

"Nobody knows what she's been to me. As much like a mother as I'd let her. I did everything but the cigarettes, and I meant to tell her I'd do that too, next month — that's her birthday."

Was this his boy, that pleading, shaken voice? He looked out: the lad was fingering Miss Strong's white apron nervously. She leaned over the railing of the little porch, her hand on his shoulder.

"You tell her about it — I'll never smoke another one. It was the last thing she asked me."

"I'll tell her — she will be so pleased, I know. She asked about you yesterday. I'll let you know as soon as I can."

Belden, a little later, hurried downstairs, with a confused idea of thanking her. On the threshold of the library he paused, amazed. Dr. Hitchcock sat before a small green baize table, studying five playing-cards held fan-shape in his left hand. Opposite him sat Miss Strong, holding the pack expectantly.

"You can give me two, my dear, I think," he said as Belden entered. Looking up, he smiled apologetically.

"I dare say you are surprised," he suggested, "but I have been much exasperated, Mr. Belden, and a long experience has taught me that nothing so quickly clears the mind as throwing a few hands of poker. Miss Strong — an invaluable person — is kindly assisting me. Did I say three? Yes, of course. Thank you. We are playing for beans only, you see."

Belden watched them curiously. She sat as imperturbably as by Caddy's bedside, her eyes fixed thoughtfully on her cards.

"— And raise you three," she said.

"Five more. You will excuse me, Belden, but your aunt, Mrs. Wetherly, is a somewhat unusually irritating woman.

I'll see you, Miss Strong—ah, yes, two pair, queens up."

"What has she done?"

"She insists that Mrs. Moore shall not only see Mr. Burchard, to which I have not the least objection, but that he shall hold a communion service, directly, there. Now, if your sister had asked for this herself, it would be another matter, but unless this is the case I always regard it as a depressing agent. It is a strain, in any case."

"I think Mrs. Moore will go through with it very easily, doctor," Miss Strong interposed, slipping the cards into their leather envelope and gathering up the beans. "She will be fresh from her nap, and it will be very short. She has promised Mrs. Wetherly, you know, and it would distress her more to break it—"

"All right, all right. Have it your way. Much obliged."

He took the cards from her and went out.

"My aunt is very trying," Belden began.

"Oh, many people feel so about it," she assured him, "especially High Church people. She only did what she thought right."

He drew a breath of relief.

"You'll see she's not too tired?" he asked; and as he went to luncheon he wondered at the comfort he derived from her mute nod.

He was roused from the table, where the dishes left by them were untouched for the most part, by a disturbance in the hall.

"It's the priest," the waitress murmured, and with a frown he checked her rising tears.

Aunt Lucia bustled through the room.

"You must come, Wilmot," she whispered eagerly, "she asked for you. Peter is locked into his room, and neither of the children has been confirmed. Susy, of course, is a Presbyterian. Not that dear Mr. Burchard would object—he is so broad. But you have no excuse. Oh, it is beautiful, Wilmot! She looks so lovely!"

He followed her wearily. What did it matter? It seemed to him ominous, terrible—but it would please Caddy. She sat propped up in the bed. Her cheeks were crimson, her eyes bright. White chrysanthemums stood in silver vases, candles burned softly on the white-draped dresser. Mr. Burchard, in the hall just beyond, was slipping his surplice over his head. A faint odor of wine mingled with the flowers.

Belden dared not look at her. She was to him, in that moment, mystic, holy, a thing apart. He dropped on his knees beside a silvery white apron, his eyes on the floor, his heart beating hard.

The clergyman entered slowly, the service began. It was all a murmured maze to him. Aunt Lucia sobbed quietly beside him, but as he glanced at her he caught a light on her wet, uplifted face that thrilled him strangely. Her deep responses spoke a faith and surety that swallowed for the moment all her little sillinesses and obstinacies.

The solemn words grew in intensity, the candles flickered audibly in the sacred hush. The clergyman moved toward the bed, and they heard Caddy's breath draw out in a deep, shuddering sob; her teeth chattered against the cup.

Belden set his jaw; it was cruel, brutal! They were killing her. His clinched fist moved blindly toward his neighbor: he touched her hand and gripped it fiercely.

In front of him on the wall hung a large photograph of Billy's base-ball nine in full uniform. He could have drawn it from memory, afterwards. Billy, he remembered, was a great catcher. He held hard to that cool, firm hand.

"—*be amongst you and remain with you always. Amen.*" There was a little stir. The hand was drawn from his.

"Come, now," whispered Aunt Lucia, and he walked, stumbling and stiff from kneeling, from the room. At the door he glanced a second backward, but only Dr. Hitchcock was to be seen, bending over the bed. Miss Strong had already taken away candles and flowers, and Caddy's triple mirror was back on the dresser.

Mr. Burchard, in his long black cassock, offered his hand cordially.

" I am glad you could be with us, Mr. Belden," he began, but the other broke in :

" If you have tired her, if this — makes a difference —" he muttered fiercely, "you will have me to settle with. Mind that ! "

He hurried down the stairs, his hands still clinched. Peter was starting off with the road-wagon. They nodded shortly at each other.

From then the time raced on incredibly. The great surgeon, with his two assistants, was in the hall ; he was on the stairs; he was lost to sight. There was a momentary rush and bustle, the closing of a door. Peter came out, whispering to himself, and disappeared somewhere. The others, clustered in the library, spoke fitfully.

"They carried her on a cot into the west room," somebody murmured close to Belden. It was little Margaret. "I saw her. She waved her hand at me! I threw her a kiss. Miss Strong smiled at me — I love Miss Strong."

Aunt Lucia sobbed. Susy bit her lip and played with Billy's unwilling hand.

"Where's my father? Where's he gone?" he demanded. "Who's that other woman with the apron?"

Miss Strong appeared at the door. "She has taken the ether very well indeed; they are much pleased," she said softly. They hung on her words, they overwhelmed her with questions. She soothed them like children.

It grew suddenly clear to Belden that Caddy would die. It must be so. He

wondered that they had hoped for anything else.   He was sorry for them all.
He watched indifferently while Miss
Strong led the children away — he knew
she was taking them to their father.
Later, while Aunt Lucia, on her knees,
read through streaming eyes from her
prayer-book, and Susy talked nervously
to him, he watched the firm, full figure
of the woman pacing up and down the
piazza outside, her arm drawn through
his restless boy's.

"God bless her!" he said aloud.

Afterwards he could never recall the con-
secutive happenings of the end.   He
saw only separate pictures.

In one, a strange young man opened
the door and said the words that frightened them with delight.

In another, a drawn, old, white-faced
man — surely not Dr. Jameson — leaned
weakly in a chair, while a woman handed
him a tiny glass of colored liquid.

In yet another, a father hid his face in his little daughter's bosom and sobbed, with shaking shoulders ; his tall son smiled bravely over the bent head.

In the last picture he himself bore a part ; for when he came upon his shy, suspicious boy clasped in the kind arms of the woman whose brown eyes, once seen, had haunted his thoughts ever since, he gathered them both to him irresistibly. As he laid his cheek against hers, he felt that it was wet with tears.

" It lies with you now," he whispered in her ear, " to give her back to us, well and strong. He says you can. Afterwards —"

She drew away from him.

" I — I must go. I am so glad — I will do my best," she answered unsteadily.

He caught her hand. " And afterwards ? " he repeated, a growing mastery in his voice. She tried to meet his eyes, but her own fell, conquered.

A PHILANTHROPIST

A PHILANTHROPIST

"I SUSPECTED him from the first," said Miss Gould, with some irritation, to her lodger. She spoke with irritation because of the amused smile of the lodger. He bowed with the grace that characterized all his lazy movements.

" He looked very much like that Tom Waters that I had at the Reformed Drunkards' League last year. I even thought he was Tom——"

"I do not know Tom?" hazarded the lodger.

"No. I don't know whether I ever mentioned him to you. He came twice to the League, and we were really quite hopeful about him, and the third time he asked to have the meeting at his house. We thought it a great sign — the best of signs, in fact. So as a great favor we went there instead of meeting at the Rooms. I was a little late — I lost the way — and when I got there I heard a great noise as if they were singing different songs at the same time. I hurried in to lead them — they get so mixed in the singing — and — it makes me blush now to think of it! — the wretch had invited them all early, and — and they were all intoxicated!

"I am sorry I told you," she added with dignity; for the lodger, in an endeavor to smile sympathetically, had lost his way and was convulsed with a mirth entirely unregretful.

"Not at all, not at all," he murmured politely. "It is a delightful story. I would not have missed it — a choir of reformed drunkards! But do you not, my dear Miss Gould, perceive in these little setbacks a warning against further attempts? Do you still attend the League? It is not possible!"

"Possible?" echoed his visitor; for owing to certain recent and untoward circumstances, Miss Gould was half reclining in her lodger's great Indian chair, sipping a glass of his '49 port. "Indeed I do! They had every one of them to be reformed all over again! It was most disgraceful!"

Her lodger checked a rising smile, and leaned solicitously toward her, regarding her firm, fine-featured face with flattering attention.

"Are you growing stronger? Can I bring you anything?" he inquired.

Miss Gould's color rose, half with anger at her weakness of body, half with a vexed consciousness of his amusement.

"Thank you, no," she returned coldly, "I am ashamed to have been so weakminded. I must go now and tell Henry to pile the wood again in the east corner. There will probably come another tramp very soon — they are very prevalent this month, I hear."

Her lodger left his low wicker seat — a proof of enormous excitement — and frowned at her.

" Do you seriously mean, Miss Gould, that you are going to run the risk of another such — such catastrophe? It is absurd. I cannot believe it of you ! Is there no other way —"

But he had been standing a long while, it occurred to him, and he retired to the chair again. A splinter of wood on his immaculate white flannel coat caught his eye, and a slow smile spread over his handsome, lazy face. It grew and grew until at last a distinct chuckle penetrated to the dusky corner where the Indian chair leaned back against dull Oriental draperies. Its occupant attempted to rise, her face stern, her mouth unrelenting. He was at her side instantly.

"Take my arm — and pardon me!" he said with an irresistible grace. "It is only my fear for your comfort, you know, Miss Gould. I cannot bear that you should be at the mercy of every drunken fellow that wishes to impose on you!"

As she crossed the hall that separated her territory from his, her fine, full figure erect, her dark head high in the air, a whimsical regret came over him that they were not younger and more foolish.

"I should certainly marry her to reform her," he said to the birch log that spluttered on his inimitable colonial fire-dogs. And then, as the remembrance of the events of the morning came to him, he laughed again.

He had been disturbed at his leisurely coffee and roll by a rapid and ceaseless pounding, followed by a violent rattling, and varied by stifled cries apparently from the woodshed. The din seemed to come from the lower part of the house, and after one or two futile appeals to the man who served as valet, cook, and butler in his bachelor establishment, he decided that he was alone in his half of the house, and that the noise came from Miss Gould's side. He strolled down the beautiful winding staircase, and dragged his crimson dressing-gown to the top of the cellar stairs, the uproar growing momentarily more terrific. Half-way down the whitewashed steps he paused, viewing the remarkable scene below him with interest and amazement. The cemented floor was literally covered with neatly chopped kindling-wood, which rose as in a tide under the efforts of a large red-faced man who, with the regularity of a machine, stooped, grasped a billet in either hand, shook them in the face of Miss Gould, who cowered upon a soap-box at his side, and flung them on the floor. From the woodhouse near the cellar muffled shouts were heard through a storm of blows on the door. From the rattling of this door, and the fact that the red-faced man aimed every third stick at it, the observer might readily conclude that some one desirous of leaving the woodhouse was locked within it.

For a moment the spectator on the stairs stood stunned. The noise was deafening ; the appearance of the man, whose expression was one of settled rage but whose actions were of the coldest regularity, was most bewildering, partially obscured as it was by the flying billets of wood ; the mechanical attempts of Miss Gould to rise from the soap-box, invariably checked by a fierce brandishing of the stick just taken from the lessening pile, were at once startling and fascinating, inasmuch as she was methodically waved back just as her knees had unbent for the trial, and as methodically essayed her escape again, alternately rising with dignity and sinking back in terror.

The red dressing-gown advanced a step, and met her gaze. Dignity and terror shifted to relief.

" Oh, Mr. Welles ! " she gasped. Her

lodger girded up his *robe de chambre* with its red silk cord and advanced with decision through the chaos of birch and hickory. A struggle, sharp but brief, and he turned to find Miss Gould offering a coil of clothes-rope with which to bind the conquered, whom conflict had sobered, for he made no resistance.

" What do you mean by such idiotic actions ? " the squire of dames demanded, as he freed the maddened Henry from his durance vile in the woodhouse and confronted the red-faced man, who had not uttered a word.

He cast a baffled glance at Miss Gould and a triumphant smile at Henry before replying. Then, disdaining the lady's righteous indignation and the hired man's threatening gestures, he faced the gentleman in the scarlet robe and spoke as man to man.

" Gov'nor," he said with somewhat thickened speech, " I come here an' I asked for a meal. An' she tol' me would

I work fer it? An' I said yes. An' she come into this ol' vault of a suller, an' she pointed to that ol' heap o' wood, an' she tol' me ter move it over ter that corner. An' I done so fer half an hour. An' I says to that blitherin' fool over there, who was workin' in that ol' wood-house, what the devil did she care w'ich corner the darned stuff was in? An' he says that she didn't care a hang, but that she'd tell the next man that come along to move it back to where I got it from; he said 'twas a matter er principle with her not to give a man a bite fer nothin'! So I shut him in his ol' house, an' w'en she come down I gave her a piece of my mind. I don't mind a little work, mis-ter, but when it come to shufflin' kind-lin's round in this ol' tomb fer half an hour an' makin' a fool o' myself fer nothin', I got my back up. My time ain't so vallyble to me as 'tis to some, gov'nor, but it's worth a damn sight more'n that!"

Miss Gould's lodger shuddered as he remembered the quarter he had surreptitiously bestowed upon the man, and the withering scorn that would be his portion were the weakness known. He smiled as he recalled the scene in the cellar when he had helped Miss Gould up the stairs and returned to soothe Henry, who regretted that he had left one timber of the woodhouse upon another.

"Though I'm bound to say, Mr. Welles, that I see how he felt. I've often felt like a fool explainin' how they was to move that wood back an' forth. It does seem strange that Miss Gould has to do it that way. Give 'em somethin' an' let 'em go, I say!"

It was precisely his own view — but how fundamentally immoral the position was he knew so well! He recalled Miss Gould's lectures on the subject, miracles of eloquence and irrefutably correct in deductions that interested him not nearly so much as the lecturer.

"So firm, so positive, so wholesome!"

he would murmur to himself in tacit apology for the instructive hours spent before their common ground, the great fireplace in the central hall. He never sat there without remembering their first interview: her resentment at an absolutely inexcusable intrusion slowly melting before his exquisite appreciation of every line and corner of the old colonial homestead; her reserve waning at every touch of his irresistible courtesy, till, to her own open amazement, she rose to conduct this connoisseur in antiquities through the rooms whose delights he had perfectly foreseen, he assured her, from the modelling of the front porch; her utter and instantaneous refusal to consider for a second his proposal to lodge a stranger in half of her father's house; and the naïve and conscientious struggle with her principles when, with a logic none the less forcible because it was so gracefully developed, he convinced her that her plain duty lay along the lines of his choice.

For as a philanthropist what could she

do ? Here were placed in her hands means she could not in conscience over-look. Rapidly translating his dollars into converts, he juggled them before her dazzled eyes ; he even hinted delicately at Duty, with that exact conception of the requirements of the stern daughter felt by none so keenly as those who systematically avoid her.

His good genius prompted him to refer casually to soup-kitchens. Now soup-kitchens were the delight of Miss Gould's heart ; toward the establishment of a soup-kitchen she had looked since the day when her father's death had left her the double legacy of his worldly goods and his unworldly philanthropy.

Visions of dozens of Bacchic revellers, riotous no more, but seated temperately each before his steaming bowl, rose to her delighted eyes ; she saw in fancy the daughters and nieces of the reformed in smiles and white aprons ladling the nu-tritious and attractive compound, earning thus an honest wage; she saw a neatly balanced account-book and a triumphant report; she saw herself the respected and deprecatory idol of a millennial village. She wavered, hesitated, and was lost.

That very evening saw the establishment of a second ménage in the north side of the house, and though a swift regret chilled her manner for weeks, she found herself little by little growing interested in her lodger, and conscious of an increasing desire to benefit him, an irritated longing to influence him for good, to turn him from the butterfly whims of a pretended invalid to an appreciation of the responsibilities of life.

For in all her well-ordered forty years Miss Gould had never seen so indolent, so capricious, so irresponsible a person. That a man of easy means, fine education, sufficient health, and gray hair should have nothing better to do than collect willow-ware and fire-irons, read the magazines, play the piano, and stroll about in the sun seemed to her nothing less than horrible.

Each day that added some new treasure to his perfectly arranged rooms, and in consequence some new song to his seductive repertoire, left a new sting in her soul. She had been influencing somebody or something all her life. She had been educating and directing and benefiting till she was forced to be grateful to that providential generosity that caused new wickedness and ignorance to spring constantly from this very soil she had cleared; for if one reform had been sufficient she would long since have been obliged to leave the little village for larger fields. She had ministered to the starved mind as to the stunted body; the idle and dissolute quaked before her. And yet here in her own household, across her hall, lived the epitome of uselessness, indolence, selfishness, and — she was forced to admit it — charm. What corresponded to a sense of humor in her caught at the discrepancy and worried over it.

What! was she not competent, then, to influence her equals? For in everything but moral stamina she was forced to admit that her lodger was her equal, if no more. Widely travelled, well read, well born, talented, handsome, deferential — but persistently amused at her, irrevocably indolent, hopelessly selfish.

With the firm intention of turning the occasions to his benefit, she had finally accepted his regular and courteous invitation to take tea with him, and had watched his graceful management of samovar and tea-cup with open disfavor. "A habit picked up in England," he had assured her, when, with the frankness characteristic of her, she had criticised him for the effeminacy. And his smiling explanation had sent a sudden flush across her smooth, firm cheeks. Was she provincial? Did she seem to him a New England villager and nothing more? She bit her lip, and the appeal she had planned went unspoken that day.

But her desire could not rest, and as to her strict notions the continual visits from her side to his seemed unsuitable, she gave in self-defence her own invitation, and Wednesday and Saturday afternoons saw her lodger across the hall drinking her own tea with wine and plum-cake by the shining kettle.

If she could command his admiration in no other way, she felt, she might safely rely on his deferential respect for the owner of that pewter tea-service — velvety, shimmering, glistening dully, with shapes that vaguely recalled Greek lamps and Etruscan urns. And she piled wedges of ambrosial plum-cake with yellow frosting on sprigged china, and set out wine in her great-grandfather's long-necked decanter, and, with what she considered a gracious tact, overlooked the flippancy of her guest's desultory conversation, and sincerely tried to discover the humorous quality in her conversation that forced a subdued chuckle now and then from her listener.

She confided most of her schemes to him, sometimes unconsciously, and grew to depend more than she knew upon his common sense and experience; for, though openly cynical of her works, he would give her what she often realized to be the best of practical advice, and his amusing generalities, though to her mind insults to humanity, had been so bitterly proved true that she looked fearfully to see his lightest adverse prophecy fulfilled.

After a cautious introduction of the subject by asking his advice as to the minimum of hours in the week one could conscientiously allow a doubtful member of the Weekly Culture Club to spend upon Browning, she endeavored to get his idea of that poet. Her famous theory as to her ability to place any one satisfactorily in the scale of culture according to his degree of appreciation of " Rabbi ben

Ezra " was unfortunately known to her lodger before she could with any verisimilitude produce the book, and he was wary of committing himself. The exquisite effrontery with which she finally brought out her gray-green volume was only equalled by the forbearing courtesy with which he welcomed both it and her.

Nor did he offer any other comment on her opening the book at a well-worn page than an apologetic removal to the only chair in the room more comfortable than the one he was at the time occupying. He listened in silence to her intelligent if somewhat sonorous rendering of selected portions of " Saul," thanking her politely at the close, and only stipulating that he should be allowed to return the favor by a reading from one of his own favorite poets. With a shocked remembrance of certain yellow-covered volumes she had often cleared away from the piazza, Miss Gould inquired if the poet in question were English. On his hearty affirmative she resigned herself with no little interest to the opportunity of seeing her way more clearly into this baffling mind, horrified at his criticism of the second reading — for she had brought the " Rabbi " forward at last.

" Then welcome each rebuff
    That turns earth's smoothness rough,
    Each sting that bids nor sit nor stand, but go ! "

she had intoned; and, fixing her eye sternly on the butterfly in white flannels, she had asked him with a telling emphasis what that meant to him? With the sweetest smile in the world, he had leaned forward, sipped his tea, gazed thoughtfully in the fire, and answered, with a polite apology for the homeliness of the illustration, that it reminded him most strongly of a tack fixed in the seat of a chair, with the attendant circumstances !

After a convulsive effort to include in one terrible sentence all the scorn and regret and pity that she felt, Miss Gould had decided that silence was best, and sat back wondering why she suffered him one instant in her parlor. He took from the floor beside him at this point a neat red volume, and, murmuring something about his inability to do the poet justice, he began to read. For one, two, four minutes Miss Gould sat staring; then she interrupted him coldly:

"And who is the author of that doggerel, Mr. Welles?"

"Edward Lear, dear Miss Gould — and a great man, too."

"I think I might have been spared—" she began with such genuine anger that any but her lodger would have quailed. He, however, merely smiled.

"But the subtlety of it — the immensity of the conception — the power of characterization!" he cried. "Just see how quietly this is treated."

And to her amazement she let him go on; so that a chance visitor, entering unannounced, might have been treated to the delicious spectacle of a charming middle-aged gentleman in white flannels reading, near a birch fire and a priceless pewter tea-service, to a handsome middle-aged woman in black silk, the following pregnant lines:

> " There was an old person of Bow,
> Whom nobody happened to know,
> So they gave him some soap,
> And said coldly, ' We hope
> You will go back directly to Bow ! '

And the illustration is worthy of the text," he added enthusiastically, as he passed the volume to her.

She had no sense of humor, but she had a sense of justice, and it occurred to her that after all an agreement was an agreement. If to listen to insinuating inanities was the price of his attention, she would pay it. She had borne more than this in order to do good.

So the readings continued, a source of

unmixed delight to her lodger and a great spiritual discipline to herself.

As the days grew milder their intimacy, profiting by the winter seclusion, led him to accompany her on her various errands. She was at first unwilling to accept his escort — it too clearly resembled a tacit consent to his idleness. But his quiet persistence, together with his evident cynicism as to the results of these professional tours, accomplished, as usual, his end ; and the wondering village might observe on hot June mornings its benefactress, languidly accompanied by a slender man in white flannels, balancing a large white green-lined umbrella, picking his way daintily along the dusty paths, with a covered basket dangling from one hand and a gray-green volume distending one white pocket.

There was material, too, for the interested observer in the picture of Miss Gould distributing reading matter, fruit, and lectures on household economy in the cottages of the mill-hands, while her lodger pitched pennies with the delighted children outside. It was on one of these occasions that Miss Gould took the opportunity to address Mr. Thomas Waters, late of the paper and cardboard manufacturing force, on the wickedness and folly of his present course of action. Mr. Waters had left his position on the strength of his wife's financial success. Mrs. Waters was a laundress, and the summer boarders, together with Mr. Welles, who alone went far toward establishing the fortunes of the family, had combined to place the head of the house in his present condition of elegant leisure.

"I wonder at you, Tom Waters, after all the interest we've taken in you! Are you not horribly ashamed to depend on your wife in this lazy way?" Miss Gould demanded of the once member of the Reformed Drunkards' League. "How many times have I explained to you that nothing — absolutely nothing — is so disgraceful as a man who will not work? What were you placed in the world for? How do you justify your existence?"

"How," replied her unabashed audience, with a wave of his pipe toward the front yard, where Mr. Welles was amiably superintending a wrestling match, "does he justify hisn?"

Had Miss Gould been less consistent and less in earnest, there were many replies open to her. As it was, she colored violently, bit her lip, made an inaudible remark, and with a bitter glance at the author of her confusion, now cheering on to the conflict the scrambling Waters children, she called their mother to account for their presence in the yard at this time on a school-day, and for the first time in her life left the house without exacting a solemn promise of amendment from the head of the family.

"I guess I fixed her that time!" Mr. Waters remarked triumphantly, as he summoned his second pair of twins from the yard and demanded of them if the gentleman had given them nickels or dimes.

The gentleman in question became uncomfortably conscious, in the course of their walk home, of an atmosphere not wholly novel, that lost no strength in this case from its studied repression. That afternoon, as they sat in the shade of the big elm, he in his flexible wicker chair, she in a straight-backed, high-seated legacy from her grandfather, the whirlwind that Mr. Waters had so lightly sown fell to the reaping of a victim too amiable and unsuspecting not to escape the sentence of any but so stern a judge as the handsome and inflexible representative of the moral order now before him.

Miss Gould was looking her best in a crisp lavender dimity, upon whose frills Mrs. Waters had bestowed the grateful exercise of her highest art. Her sleek, dark coils of hair, from which no one stray lock escaped, framed her fresh cheeks most admirably ; her strong white hands appeared and disappeared with an absolute regularity through the dark-green wool out of which she was evolving a hideous and useful shawl. To her lodger, who alternately waved a palm-leaf fan and drank lemonade, reading at intervals from a two-days-old newspaper, and carrying on the desultory and amusing soliloquy that they were pleased to consider conversation, she presented the most attractive of pictures. " So firm, so positive, so wholesome," he murmured to himself, calling her attention to the exquisite effect of the slanting rays that struck the lawn in a dappled pattern of flickering leaf-shadows, and remarking the violet tinge thrown by the setting sun on the old spire below in the middle of the village. She did not answer immediately, and when she did it was in tones that he had learned from various slight experiments to regard as final.

"Mr. Welles," she said, bending upon him that direct and placid regard that rendered evasion difficult and paltering impossible, "things have come to a point"; and she narrated the scene of the morning.

"It is indeed a problem," observed her lodger gravely, "but what is one to do? It is just such questions as this that illustrate the futility—"

"There is no question about it, Mr. Welles," she interrupted gravely. "Tom was right and I was wrong. There is no use in my talking to him or anybody while I — while you — while things are as they are. You must make up your mind, Mr. Welles."

"But, great heavens, dear Miss Gould, what do you mean? What am I to make up my mind about? Am I to provide myself with an occupation, perhaps, for the sake of Tom Waters's principles? Or am I—"

"Yes. That is just it. You know

what I have always felt, Mr. Welles, about it. But I never seemed to be able to make you see. Now, as I say, things have come to a point. You must do something."

" But this is absurd, Miss Gould! I am not a child, and surely nobody can dream of holding you in any way responsible — "

" *I* hold myself responsible," she replied simply, "and I have never approved of it — never!"

He shrugged his shoulders desperately. She was imperturbable; she was impossible; she was beyond argument or persuasion or ridicule.

"Suppose I say that I think the situation is absurd, and that I refuse to be placed at Mr. Waters's disposal?" he suggested with a furtive glance. She drew the ivory hook through the green meshes a little faster.

" I should be obliged to refuse to re-

new your lease in the fall," she answered.
He started from his wicker chair.

"You cannot mean it, Miss Gould!
You would not be so—so unkind, so
unjust!"

"I should feel obliged to, Mr. Welles,
and I should not feel unjust."

He sank back into the yielding chair
with a sigh. After all, her fascination
had always lain in her great decision.
Was it not illogical to expect her to fail to
display it at such a crisis? There was a
long silence. The sun sank lower and
lower, the birds twittered happily around
them. Miss Gould's long white hook
slipped in and out of the wool, and her
lodger's eyes followed it absently. After
a while he rose, settled his white jacket
elaborately, and half turned as if to go
back to the house.

"I need not tell you how I regret this
unfortunate decision of yours," he said
politely, with a slight touch of the hauteur

that sat so well on his graceful person. "I can only say that I am sorry you yourself should regret it so little, and that I hope it will not disturb our pleasant acquaintance during the weeks that remain to me."

She bowed slightly with a dignified gesture that often served her as a reply, and he took a step toward her.

"Would we not better come in?" he suggested. "The sun is gone, and your dress is thin. Let me send Henry after the chairs," and his eyes dropped to her hands again. They were nearly hidden by the green wool, but the long needle quivered like a leaf in the wind; she could not pass it between the thread and her white forefinger. He hesitated a moment, glanced at her face, smiled inscrutably, and deliberately reseated himself.

"What in the world could I do, you see?" he inquired meditatively, as if that had been the subject under discussion for some time. "I can't make cardboard boxes, you know. It's perfectly useless, my going into a factory. Wheels and belts and things always give me the maddest longing to jump into them — I couldn't resist it! And that would be so unpleasant —"

She dropped her wool and clasped her hands under it.

"Oh, Mr. Welles," she cried eagerly, "how absurd! As if I meant that! As if I meant anything like it!"

"Had you thought of anything, then?" he asked interestedly.

She nodded gravely. "Why, yes," she said. "It wouldn't be right for me to say you must do something, and then offer no suggestions whatever, knowing as I do how you feel about it. I thought of such a good plan, and one that would be the best possible answer to Tom —"

"Oh, good heavens!" murmured her lodger, but she went on quickly: "You know I was going to open the soup-kitchen in October. Well, I've just thought, Why not get the Rooms all ready, and the reading-room moved over there, and have lemonade and sandwiches and sarsaparilla, and Kitty Waters to begin to serve right away, as she's beginning to run the streets again, and Annabel Riley with her? Then the Civic Club can have its headquarters there, and people will begin to be used to it before cold weather."

" And I am to serve sarsaparilla and sandwiches with Kitty and Annabel? Really, dear Miss Gould, if you knew how horribly ill sarsaparilla is certain to make me — I have loathed it from childhood—"

"Oh, no, no, no!" she interrupted, with her sweet, tolerant smile. She smiled at him as if he had been a child.

"You know I never meant that you should work all day, Mr. Welles. It isn't at all necessary. I have always felt that an hour or two a day of intelligent, cultivated work was fully equal to a much longer space of manual labor that is more mechanical, more tiresome."

"Better fifty years of poker than a cycle of croquet!" her lodger murmured. "Yes, I have always felt that myself."

"And somebody must be there from ten to twelve, say, in the mornings, in what we call the office; just to keep an eye on things, and answer questions about the kitchen, and watch the reading-room, and recommend the periodicals, and take the children's Civic League reports, and oversee the Rooms generally. Now I'd be there Wednesdays to meet the mothers, and Mrs. Underwood Saturdays for the Band of Hope and the kitchen-garden. It would be just Mondays, Tuesdays, Thursdays, and Fridays from ten to twelve, say!"

"From ten to twelve, say," he repeated absently, with his eyes on her handsome, eager face. He had never seen her so animated, so girlishly insistent. She urged with the vivid earnestness of twenty years.

"My dear lady," he brought out finally, "you are like Greek architecture or Eastlake furniture or — or 'God Save the Queen' — perfectly absolute! And I am so hideously relative — But, after all, why should a sense of humor be an essential? One is really more complete — I suppose Mahomet had none — When shall I begin?"

The interested villagers were informed early and regularly of the progress of the latest scheme of their benefactress. Henry and Mr. Waters furnished most satisfactory and detailed bulletins to gatherings of leisurely and congenial spirits, who listened with incredulous amazement to the accounts of Mr. Welles's proceedings.

"Him an' that hired man o' his, they have took more stuff over to them Rooms than you c'd shake a stick at! I never see nothing like it — never! Waxed that

floor, they have, and put more mats onto
it — fur and colored. An' the stuff —
oh, Lord! China — all that blue china
he got fr'm ol' Mis' Simms, an' them ol'
stoneware platters that Mis' Rivers was
goin' to fire away, an' he give her two
dollars for the lot — all that's scattered
round on tables and shelves. An' that
ol' black secr'tary he got fr'm Lord
knows where, an' brakes growin' in colored pots standin' right up there, an'
statyers o' men an' women — no heads
onto 'em, some ain't got; it's all one
to him — he'd buy any ol' thing so's
'twas broke, you might say. An' them
ol' straight chairs — no upholsterin' on
'em, an' some o' them wicker kind that
bends any way, with pillers in 'em. An'
cups and sassers, with a tea-pot 'n' -kittle;
an' he makes tea himself an' drinks it —
I swear it's so. An' a guitar, an', Lord,
the pictures! You can't see no wall for
'em!

"'It's a mighty lucky thing, havin'

this room, Thompson,' says he to that hired man, 'the things was spillin' over. We'll make it a bower o' beauty, Thompson,' says he. 'Yes, sir,' says the man. That's all he ever says, you might say. I never see nothin' like it, never, the way that hired man talks to him; you'd think he was the Queen o' Sheba.

"An' he goes squintin' about here an' there, changin' this an' that, an' singin' away an' laughin'—you'd think he'd have a fit. Seems's if he loved to putter about 'n' fool with things in a room, like women. I heard him say so myself. I was helpin' Miss Gould with the other rooms—she ain't seen his; she don't know no more'n the dead what he's got in there—an' I was by the door when he said it.

"'Thompson,' says he, 'if I don't keep my present situation,' says he, 'I c'n go out as a decorator an' furnisher. Don't you think I'd succeed, Thompson?' says he. 'Yes, sir,' says Thompson.

"'You see, we've got to do somethin', Thompson,' says he. 'We've got ter justify our existence, Thompson,' an' he commenced to laugh. 'Yes, sir,' says Thompson. Beats all I ever see, the way that man answers back!'"

An almost unprecedented headache, brought on by her unremitting labor in effecting the change in the Rooms, kept Miss Gould in the house for two days after the new headquarters had been satisfactorily arranged; and as Mr. Welles had refused to open his office for inspection till it was completely furnished, she did not enter that characteristic apartment till the third day of its official existence.

As she went through the narrow hallway connecting the four rooms on which the social regeneration of her village depended, she caught the sweet low thrum of a guitar and a too familiarly seductive voice burst forth into a chant, whose literal significance she was unable to grasp, owing to lack of familiarity with the language in which it was couched, but whose general tenor no one could mistake, so tender and arch was the rendering.

With a vague thrill of apprehension she threw open the door.

Sunk in cushions, a tea-cup on the arm of his chair, a guitar resting on his white flannel sleeve, reclined the director of the Rooms. Over his head hung a large and exquisite copy of the Botticelli Venus. Miss Gould's horrified gaze fled from this work of art to rest on a representation in bronze of the same reprehensible goddess, clothed, to be sure, a little more in accordance with the views of a retired New England community, yet leaving much to be desired in this direction. Kitty Waters attentively filled his empty cup, beaming the while, and the once errant Annabel, sitting on a low stool at his feet, with a red bow in her pretty hair, and her great brown eyes fixed adoringly on his face as he directed the fascinating incomprehensible little song straight at her charming self, was obviously in no present danger of running the streets.

"Good morning, Miss Gould!" he said cheerfully, rising and handing the guitar to the abashed Annabel. "And you are really quite recovered? *C'est bien!* Business is dull, and we are amusing each other, you see. How do you like the rooms? I flatter myself—"

"If you flattered none but yourself, Mr. Welles, much harm would be avoided," she interrupted with uncompromising directness. "Kitty and Annabel, I cannot see how you can possibly tell how many people may or may not be wanting lunch!"

"Billy Rider tells us when any one comes," the director assured her. "They don't come till twelve, anyway, and then they want to see the room, mostly—

which we show them, don't we, Annabel?"

Annabel blushed, cast down her eyes, lifted them, showed her dimples, and replied in the words, if not in the accents, of Thompson: "Yes, sir!"

"It's really going to be an education in itself, don't you think so?" he continued. "It's amazing how the people like it — it's really quite gratifying. Perhaps it may be my mission to abolish the chromo and the tidy from off the face of New England! We have had crowds here — just to look at the pictures."

"I don't doubt it!" replied Miss Gould briefly.

"And I got the most attractive sugar-bowl from the little boy who brought in the reports about picking up papers and such things from the streets. He said he ought to have five cents, so I gave him a dime — I hadn't five — and I bought the bowl. Annabel, my child, bring me —"

But Annabel and her fellow-waitress had disappeared. Miss Gould sat in silence. At intervals her perplexed gaze rested unconsciously on the Botticelli Venus, from which she instantly with a slight frown lowered it and regarded the floor. When she at last met his eyes the expression of her own was so troubled, the droop of her firm mouth so pathetic and unusual, that he left his chair and dragged the little stool to her feet, assuming an attitude so boyish and graceful that in spite of herself she smiled at him.

"What is the matter?" he asked confidentially. "Is anything wrong? Don't you like the room? I enjoy it tremendously, myself. I've been here almost all the time since it was done. I think Tom Waters must be tremendously impressed —"

"That's the trouble; he is," said Miss Gould simply.

"Trouble? trouble? Is his impression unfavorable ? Heavens, how unfortunate ! " exclaimed the director airily. " Surely, my application — Does the room fail to meet his approval, or —"

" Yes, it does," she interrupted. " He says it's no place for a man to be in ; and he says the pictures are — are — well, he says they are improper ! " glancing at the Venus.

" Ah ! " responded the director with a suspicious sweetness. " He does not care for the nude, then ? "

She sighed deeply. " Oh, Mr. Welles ! "

" It is indeed to be regretted that Mr. Waters's ideals are so high — and — shall we say — so elusive ? " proceeded the director smoothly. " It is so difficult — so well-nigh impossible — to satisfy him. One devotes one's energies — I may say one slaves night and day — to win some slight mark of approval ; and just as one is about to reap the well-earned reward — a smile, a word of appreciation — all is forfeited ! It is hard indeed ! Would you suggest the rearrangement of the Rooms under Mr. Waters's direction? Thompson is at his service —"

"Oh, Mr. Welles!" she sighed hopelessly. "It isn't only that! It's not alone the room, though Mrs. Underwood wonders that I should think she would be able to conduct the Band of Hope in here, and Mrs. Rider says that after what her husband told her she should no more think of sitting here for a mothers' meeting than anything in the world. It's the whole thing. Why did you treat them all to lemonade the first day? Surely you knew that our one aim is to prevent miscellaneous charity. And Tom says you smoked in here — he smelt it."

"I smelt him, too," remarked the director calmly. "That was one reason why I smoked."

"And — and having Kitty and Annabel here all the time! The Girls' Club are so j — Well, the Girls' Club like the old rooms better, they say, and it's so difficult to get them to work together at best.   And now we shall have to work so hard —

"And the men think it's just a joke, the lemonade and everything, and the room gave them such a wrong impression, and they don't seem to want it, anyway. Tom Waters says he can't abide sarsaparilla — "

" Great heavens!" the director broke in, " is it possible? A point on which Mr. Waters's opinion coincides with mine? I have not lived in vain! But this is too much; I have not deserved — "

"Oh, don't!" she begged. " There is more. When I corrected Annabel for what I had heard about her — her impertinent behavior, she said that Mrs. Underwood had never approved of the whole thing, and that if I had consulted her she would never have given her consent to your being here, and that I was dictatorial — I !"

Her lodger coughed and ejaculated, "You, indeed!"

"And when I said that their ingratitude actually made me wonder why I worked so hard for them, she said — oh, dear! It is all dreadful! I don't know what to do!"

"I do!" returned her lodger promptly. "Go away and leave 'em! They aren't fit to trouble you any more. Besides, they're really not so bad, after all, you know. There has to be just about so much laziness and — and that sort of thing, don't you see. Look at me, for instance! Think of how much misdirected energy I balance! And it gives other people something to do. . . . Go away and leave it all for a while!" he repeated smilingly.

"Go away! But where? Why should I? What do you mean?" she stammered, confused at something in his eyes, which never left her face.

"To England — you said you'd like

to see it. With me — for I certainly couldn't stay here alone. Why do you suppose I stay, dear lady? I used to wonder myself. No, sit still, don't get up! I am about to make you an offer of marriage; indeed, I am serious, Miss Gould!

" I don't see that it's ridiculous at all. I see every practical reason in favor of it. In the first place, if they are gossiping — oh, yes, Thompson told me, and I wonder that they hadn't before: these villages are dreadful places — I couldn't very well stay, you see; and then where should I put all my things? In the second place, I have so much stuff, and there's no house fit for it but—but ours; and if we were married I could have just twice as much room for it — and I'm getting far too much for my side. In the third place, I find that I can't look forward with any pleasure to travelling about alone, because, in the fourth place, I've grown so tremendously fond of you, dear Miss Gould! I think you don't dislike me?"

She plucked the guitar strings nervously with her white, strong fingers. The rich, vibrating tones of it filled the room and confused her still more.

"People will say that I — that we —" He caught her hand: it had never been kissed before. "Would you rather I went away and then there would be nothing left for them to say?" he asked softly.

She caught her breath.

"I'm too — "

"You are too charming not to have some one who appreciates the fact as thoroughly as I do," he interrupted gallantly. "I think you do me so much good, you know," he added, still holding her hand. She looked at him directly for the first time.

"Do I really? Is that true?" she demanded, with a return of her old manner so complete and sudden as to startle him. "If I thought that — "

"You would?" he asked with a smile. "I thought so! Here is a village that scorns your efforts and a respectful suitor who implores them. Can you hesitate?"

His smile was irresistible, and she returned it half reprovingly. "Will you never be serious?" she said. "I wonder that I can——" She stopped.

"That you can——" he repeated, watching her blush, but she would not finish.

"You must not think that I can give up my work—my real work—so easily," she said, rising and looking down on him with a return of her simple impressive seriousness. "I shall have to consider. I have been very much disturbed by their conduct. I will see you after supper," and with a gesture that told him to remain, she left the room, her head high as she caught Annabel's voice from outside. She turned in the door, however, and the stern curves of her mouth melted with a smile so sweet, a promise so gracious and so tender, that when her eyes, frank and direct as a boy's, left his, he looked long at the closed door, wondering at the quickening of his pulses.

A moment later he heard her voice, imperious and clear, and the mumble of Mr. Waters's unavailing if never-ending excuses. He laughed softly to himself, and touched the strings of the guitar that she had struck. "I shall save the worthy Thomas much," he murmured to himself, "and of course I do it to reform her—I cannot pull down the village and die with the Philistines!"

She went up the long main street, Mr. Waters at her side and Annabel Riley behind her. Her lodger watched her out of sight, and prepared to lock up the Rooms.

"So firm, so positive, so wholesome!" he said, as he started after her.

A REVERSION TO TYPE

A REVERSION TO TYPE

SHE had never felt so tired of it all, it seemed to her. The sun streamed hot across the backs of the shining seats into her eyes, but she was too tired to get the window-pole. She watched the incoming class listlessly, wondering whether it would be worth while to ask one of them to close the shutter. They chattered and giggled and bustled in, rattling the chairs about, and begging one another's pardon vociferously, with that insistent politeness which marks a sharply defined stage in the social evolution of the young girl. They irritated her excessively — these little airs and graces. She opened her book with a snap, and began to call the roll sharply.

Midway up the room sat a tall, dark girl, not handsome, but noticeably well dressed. She looked politely at her questioner when spoken to, but seemed as far in spirit as the distant trees toward which she directed her attention when not particularly addressed. She seemed to have a certain personality, a self-possession, a source of interest other than collegiate; and this held her apart from the others in the mind of the woman who sat before the desk.

What was that girl thinking of, she wondered, as she called another name and glanced at the book to gather material for a question. What a perfect taste had combined that dark, brocaded vest with the dull, rough cloth of the suit — and she dressed her hair so well! She had a beautiful band of pearls on one finger: was it an engagement-ring? No, that would be a solitaire.

And all this time she called names from the interminable list, and mechanically corrected the mistakes of their owners. Her eyes went back to the girl in the middle row, who turned her head and yawned a little. They took their education very easily, these maidens.

How she had saved and denied herself, and even consented to the indebtedness she so hated, to gain that coveted German winter! And how delightful it had been!

Almost she saw again the dear home of that blessed year: the kindly house-mother; the chubby *Mädchen*, who knitted her a silk purse, and cried when she left; the father with his beloved 'cello and his deep, honest voice.

How cunning the little Bertha had been! How pleasant it was to hear her gay little voice when one came down the shady street! "*Da ist sie, ja!*" she would call to her mother, and then Hermann would come up to her with his hands outstretched. Had she had a hard day? Was the lecture good? How brown his beard was, and how deep and faithful his brown eyes were! And he used to sing — why were there no bass voices in the States? "*Kennst du das Land*," he used to sing, and his mother cried softly to herself for pleasure. And once she herself had cried a little.

"No," she said to the girl who was reciting, "no, it takes the dative. I cannot seem to impress sufficiently on your minds the necessity for learning that list thoroughly. You may translate now."

And they translated. How they drawled it over, the beautiful, rich German. Hermann had begged so, but she had felt differently then. She had loved her work in anticipation. To marry and settle down — she was not ready. It would be so good to be independent. And now — But it was too late. That was years ago. Hermann must have found some yellow-braided, blue-eyed Dorothea by this —

some *Mädchen* who cared not for calculus and Hebrew, but only to be what her mother had been, wife and house-mother. But this was treason. Our grandmothers had thought that.

She looked at the girl in the middle row. What beautiful hair she had! What an idiot she was to give up four years of her life to this round of work and play and pretence of living! Oh, to go back to Germany — to see Bertha and her mother again, and hear the father's 'cello! Hermann had loved her so! He had said, so quietly and yet so surely: "But thou wilt come back, my heart's own. And always I wait here for thee. Make me not wait long!" He had seemed too quiet then — too slow and too easily content. She had wanted quicker, busier, more individual life. And now her heart said, "O fool!"

Was it too late? Suppose she should go, after all? Suppose she should go, and all should be as it had been, only a little older, a little more quiet and peaceful? The very fancy filled her heart with sudden calm. A love so deep and sure, so broad and sweet — could it not dignify any woman's life? And she had been thought worthy and had refused this love! O fool!

Suppose she went and found — her heart beat too quickly, and her face flushed. She called on the bright girl in the front row.

"And what have *you* learned?" she said.

The girl coughed importantly. "It is a poem of Goethe's," she announced in her high, satisfied voice. "*Kennst du das Land —*"

"That will do," said the German assistant. "I fear we shall not have time for it to-day. The hour is up. You may go on with the translation for to-morrow." And as the class rose with a growing clamor she realized that though she had been thinking steadily in German, she had been talking in English. So that was why they had comprehended so well and answered so readily! And yet she was too glad to be annoyed at the slip. There were other things: her life was not a German class!

As the girls crowded out, one stopped by the desk. She laid her hand with the pearl band on the third finger on the teacher's arm. "You look tired," she said. "I hope you're not ill?"

"Ill?" said the woman at the desk. "I never felt better. I've been neglecting my classes, I fear, in the study of your green gown. It is so very pretty."

The girl smiled and colored a little.

"I'm glad you like it," she said. "I like it, too." Then, with a sudden feeling of friendship, an odd sense of intimacy, a quick impulse of common femininity, she added:

"I've had some good times in this dress. Wearing it up here makes me remember them very strangely. It's queer, what a difference it makes—" She stopped and looked questioningly at the older woman.

But the German assistant smiled at her. "Yes," she said, "it is. And when you have been teaching seven years the difference becomes very apparent." She gathered up her books, still smiling in a reminiscent way. And as she went out of the door, she looked back at the glaring, sunny room as if already it were far behind her, as if already she felt the house-mother's kiss, and heard the 'cello, and saw Klara's tiny daughter standing by the door, throwing kisses, calling, "*Da ist sie, ja!*"

Lost in the dream, her eyes fixed absently, she stumbled against her fellow-assistant, who was making for the room she had just left.

"I beg your pardon — I wasn't looking. Oh, it's you!" she murmured vaguely. Her fellow-assistant had a headache, and forty-five written papers to correct. She had just heard, too, a cutting criticism of her work made by the self-appointed faculty critic; the criticism was cleverly worded, and had just enough truth to fly quickly and hurt her with the head of her department. So she was not in the best of tempers.

"Yes, it's I," she said crossly. "If you had knocked these papers an inch farther, I should have invited you to correct them. If you go about in that abstracted way much longer, my dear, Miss Selbourne will inform the world (on the very best authority) that you're in love."

"I? What nonsense!"

It was a ridiculous thing to say, and she flushed angrily at herself. It was only a joke, of course.

The other woman laughed shortly.

"Dear me! I really believe you are!" she exclaimed. "The girls were saying at breakfast that Professor Tredick was ruining himself in violets yesterday — so it was for you!" and she went into the lecture-room.

A chattering crowd of girls closed in behind her. One voice rose above the rest:

"Well, I don't know what you call it, then. He skated with her all the winter, and at the Dickinson party they sat on one sofa for an hour and talked steadily!"

"Oh, nonsense! She skates beautifully, that's all."

"She sits on a sofa beautifully, too." A burst of laughter, and the door closed.

The German assistant smiled satirically. It was all of a piece. At least, the younger women were perfectly frank about it: they did not feel themselves forced to employ sarcasm in their references; it was not necessary for them to appear to have definitely chosen this life in preference to any other. Four years was little to lend to such an experiment. But the older women, who sat on those prim little platforms year after year — a sudden curiosity possessed her to know how many of them were really satisfied.

Could it be that they had preferred —
actually preferred — But she had, herself,
three years ago. She shook her head
decidedly. "Not for nine years, not for
nine!" she murmured, as she caught
through the heavy door a familiar voice
raised to emphasize some French phrase.

And yet, somebody must teach them.
They could not be born with foreign
idioms and historical dates and mathe-
matical formulæ in their little heads.
She herself deplored the modern tendency
that sent a changing drift of young teachers through the colleges, to learn at the
expense of the students a soon relinquished
profession. But how ridiculous the position of the women who prided themselves
on the steadiness and continuity of their
service! Surely they must find it an empty
success at times. They must regret.

She was passing through the chapel.
Two scrubbing-women were straightening
the chairs, their backs turned to her.

"From all I hear," said one, with a

chuckle and a sly glance, "we'll be afther gettin' our invitations soon."

"An' to what?" demanded the other quickly.

"Sure, they say it's a weddin'."

"Ah, now, hush yer noise, Mary Nolan; 'tis no such thing. I've had enough o' husbands. I know when I'm doin' well, an' that's as I am!"

"'Tis strange that the men sh'd think different, now, but they do!"

They laughed heartily and long. The German assistant looked at the broad backs meditatively. Just now they seemed to her more consistent than any other women in the great building.

She walked quickly across the greening campus. The close-set brick buildings seemed to press up against her; every window stood for some crowded, narrow room, filled with books and tea-cups and clothes and photographs — hundreds of them, and all alike. In her own room she tried to reason herself out of this intolerable depression, to realize the advantages of a quiet life in what was surely the same pleasant, cultured atmosphere to which she had so eagerly looked forward three years ago. Her room was large, well furnished, perfectly heated ; and if the condition of her closet would have appeared nothing short of appalling to a householder, that condition was owing to the hopeless exigencies of the occasion. With the exception of that whited sepulchre, all was neat, artistic, eminently habitable. She surveyed it critically : the " Mona Lisa," the large " Melrose Abbey," the Burne-Jones draperies, and the " Blessed Damozel " that spread a placid if monotonous culture through the rooms of educated single women. A proper appreciation of polished wood, the sanitary and æsthetic values of the open fire, a certain scheme in couch-pillows, all linked it to the dozen other rooms that occupied the same relative ground-floor corners in a dozen other houses. Some of them had more books, some ran to handsome photographs, some afforded fads in old furniture; but it was only a question of more or less. It looked utterly impersonal to-day; its very atmosphere was artificial, typical, a pretended self-sufficiency.

How many years more should she live in it — three, nine, thirteen? The tide of girls would ebb and flow with every June and September; eighteen to twenty-two would ring their changes through the terms, and she could take her choice of the two methods of regarding them: she could insist on a perennial interest in the separate personalities, and endure weariness for the sake of an uncertain influence; or she could mass them frankly as the student body, and confine the connection to marking their class-room efforts and serving their meat in the dining-room. The latter was at once more honest and more easy; all but the most ambitious or the most conscientious came to it sooner or later.

The youngest among the assistants, themselves fresh from college, mingled naturally enough with the students; they danced and skated and enjoyed their girlish authority. The older women, seasoned to the life, settled there indefinitely, identified themselves more or less with the town, amused themselves with their little aristocracy of precedence, and wove and interwove the complicated, slender strands of college gossip. But a woman of barely thirty, too old for friendships with young girls, too young to find her placid recreation in the stereotyped round of social functions, that seemed so perfectly imitative of the normal and yet so curiously unsuccessful at bottom—what was there for her?

Her eyes were fixed on the hill-slope view that made her room so desirable. It occurred to her that its changelessness was not necessarily so attractive a characteristic as the local poets practised themselves in assuring her.

A light knock at the door recalled to

her the utter lack of privacy that put her at the mercy of laundress, sophomore, and expressman. She regretted that she had not put up the little sign whose "*Please do not disturb*" was her only means of defence.

"Come!" she called shortly, and the tall girl in the green dress stood in the open door. A strange sense of long acquaintance, a vague feeling of familiarity, surprised the older woman. Her expression changed.

"Come in," she said cordially.

"I—am I disturbing you?" asked the girl doubtfully. She had a pile of books on her arm; her trim jacket and hat, and something in the way she held her armful, seemed curiously at variance with her tam-o'-shantered, golf-caped friends.

"I couldn't find out whether you had an office hour, and I didn't know whether I ought to have sent in my name — it seemed so formal, when it is only a moment I need to see you —"

"Sit down," said the German assistant pleasantly. "What can I do for you?"

"I have been talking with Fräulein Müller about my German, and she says if you are willing to give me an outline for advanced work and an examination later on, I can go into a higher division in a little while. Languages are always easy for me, and I could go on much quicker."

"Oh, certainly. I have thought more than once that you were wasting your time. The class is too large and too slow. I will make you out an outline and give it to you after class to-morrow," said the German assistant promptly. "Meanwhile, won't you stay and make me a little call? I will light the fire and make some tea, if that is an inducement."

"The invitation is inducement enough, I assure you," smiled the girl, "but I must not stay to-day, I think. If you will let me come again, when I have no work to bother you with, I should love to."

There was something easily decisive in her manner, something very different from the other students, who refused such invitations awkwardly, eager to be pressed, and when finally assured of a sincere welcome, prolonged their calls and talked about themselves into the uncounted hours. Evidently she would not stay this time; evidently she would like to come again.

As the door closed behind her the German assistant dropped her cordial smile and sank back listlessly in her chair.

"After all, she's only a girl!" she murmured. For almost an hour she sat looking fixedly at the unlit logs, hardly conscious of the wasted time. Much might have gone into that hour. There was tea for her at one of the college houses—the hostess had a "day," and went so far as to aspire to the exclusive serving of a certain kind of tinned fancy biscuit every Friday—if she wanted to drop in. This hostess invited favored students to meet the faculty and towns-people on these occasions, and the two latter classes were expected to effect a social fusion with the former — which linked it, to some minds, a little too ob-viously with professional duties.

She might call on the head of her de-partment, who was suffering from some slight indisposition, and receive minute advice as to the conduct of her classes, mingled with general criticism of various colleagues and their methods. She might make a number of calls; but if there is one situation in which the futility of these social mockeries becomes most thoroughly obvious, it is the situation presented by an attempt to imitate the conventional society life in a woman's college. And yet — she had gone over the whole ques-tion so often — what a desert of awk-wardness and learned provincialism such a college would be without the attempt! How often she had cordially agreed to the statement that it was precisely because of its insistence upon this connection with the forms and relations of normal life that her college was so successfully free from the tomboyishness or the priggishness or the gaucherie of some of the others ! And yet its very success came from begging the question, after all.

She shook her head impatiently. A strong odor of boiling chocolate crept through the transom. Somebody began to practise a monotonous accompaniment on the guitar. Over her head a series of startling bumps and jarring falls suggested a troupe of baby elephants practising for their first appearance in public. The German assistant set her teeth.

" Before I die," she announced to her image in the glass, " I propose to inquire flatly of Miss Burgess if she *does* pile her furniture in a heap and slide down it on her toboggan ! There is no other logical explanation of that horrible disturbance."

The face in the glass caught her attention. It looked sallow, with lines under the eyes. The hair rolled back a little too severely for the prevailing mode, and she recalled her late visitor's effectively adjusted side-combs, her soft, dark waves.

"They have time for it, evidently," she mused, "and after all it is certainly more important than modal auxiliaries!"

And for half an hour she twisted and looped and coiled, between the chiffonnier and a hand-glass, fairly flushing with pleasure at the result.

"Now," she said, looking cheerfully at a pile of written papers, "I'll take a walk, I think — a real walk." And till dinner-time she tramped some of the old roads of her college days — more girlish than those days had found her, lighter-footed, she thought, than before.

The flush was still in her cheeks as she served her hungry tableful, and she could not fail to catch the meaning of their frank stares. Pausing in the parlor door to answer a question, she overheard a bit of conversation :

"Doesn't she look well with her hair low? Quite stunning, I think."

"Yes, indeed. If only she wouldn't dress so old! It makes her look older than she is. That red waist she wears in the evening is awfully becoming."

"Yes, I hate her in dark things."

The regret that she had not found time to put on the red waist was so instant and keen that she laughed at herself when alone in her room. She moved vaguely about, aimlessly changing the position of the furniture. How absurd! To do one's hair differently, and take a long walk, and feel as if an old life were somehow far behind one!

Later she found herself before her desk, hunting for her foreign letter-paper, and once started, her pen flew. There were long meditative lapses, followed by nervous haste, as if to make up the lost time; and just before the ten-o'clock bell she slipped out to mail a fat brown-stamped envelope. The night-watchman chuckled as he watched the head shrouded in the golf-cape hood bend a moment over the little white square.

"Maybe it's one o' the maids, maybe it's one o' the teachers, maybe it's one o' the girls," he confided to his lantern; "they're all alike, come to that! An' a good thing, too!"

In the morning the German assistant dismissed her last class early and took train for Springfield. On the way to the station a deferential clerk from the book-shop waylaid her.

"One moment, please. Those books you spoke of. Mr. Hartwell's library is up at auction and we're sending a man to buy to-day. If you could get the whole set for twenty-five dollars—"

She smiled and shook her head. "I've changed my mind, thank you — I can't afford it. Yes, I suppose it is a bargain, but books are such a trouble to carry about, you know. No, I don't think of anything else."

What freedom, what a strange baseless exhilaration! Suppose — suppose it was all a mistake, and she should wake back to the old stubborn, perfunctory reality! Perhaps it was better, saner — that quiet taken-for-granted existence. Perhaps she regretted — but even with the half-fear at her heart she laughed at that. If wake she must, she loved the dream. How she trusted that man! "Always I will wait"—and he would. But seven years! She threw the thought behind her.

The next days passed in a swift, confused flight. She knew they were all discussing her, wondering at her changed face, her fresh, becoming clothes; they decided that she had had money left her.

"Some of my girls saw you shopping in Springfield last Saturday — they say you got some lovely waists," said her fellow-assistant tentatively. "Was this one? It's very sweet. You ought to wear red a great deal, you look so well in it. Did you know Professor Riggs spoke of your hat with wild enthusiasm to Mrs. Austin Sunday? He said it was wonderful what a difference a stylish hat made. Not that he meant, of course — Well, it's lovely to be able to get what you want. Goodness knows, I wish I could."

The other laughed. "Oh, it's perfectly easy if you really want to," she said, "it all depends on what you want, you know."

For the first week she moved in a kind of exaltation. It was partly that her glass showed her a different woman : soft-eyed, with cheeks tinted from the long, restless walks through the spring that was coming on with every warm, greening day. The excitement of the letter hung over her. She pictured her announcement, Fräulein Müller's amazed questions.

"'But—but I do not understand! You are not well?'

"'Perfectly, thank you.'

"'But I am perfectly satisfied: I do not wish to change. You are not sick, then?'

"'Only of teaching, Fräulein.'

"'But the instructorship—I was going to recommend—do not be alarmed; you shall have it surely!'

"'You are very kind, but I have taught long enough.'

"'Then you do not find another position? Are you to be—'"

Always here her heart sank. Was she? What real basis had all this sweet, disturbing dream? To write so to a man after seven years! It was not decent. She grew satiric. How embarrassing for him to read such a letter in the bosom of an affectionate, flaxen-haired family! At least, she would never know how he really felt, thank Heaven. And what was left for her then? To her own mind she had burned her bridges already. She was as far from this place in fancy as if the miles stretched veritably between them. And yet she knew no other life. She knew no other men. He was the only one. In a flash of shame it came over her that a woman with more experience would never have written such a letter. Everybody knew that men forget, change, easily replace first loves. Nobody but such a cloistered, academic spinster as she would have trusted a seven years' promise. This was another result of such lives as they led — such helpless, provincial women. Her resentment grew against the place. It had made her a fool.

It was Sunday afternoon, and she had omitted, in deference to the day, the short skirt and walking-hat of her week-day stroll. Sunk in accusing shame, her cheeks flaming under her wide, dark hat, her quick step more sweeping than she knew, her eyes on the ground, she just escaped collision with a suddenly looming masculine figure. A hasty apology, a startled glance of appeal, a quick breath that parted her lips, and she was past the stranger. But not before she had caught in his eyes a look that quickened her heart, that soothed her angry humility. The sudden sincere admiration, the involuntary tribute to her charm, was new to her, but the instinct of countless generations made it as plain and as much her prerogative as if she had been the most successful débutante. She was not, then, an object of pity, to be treasured for the sake of the old days; other men, too — the impulse outstripped thought, but she caught up with it.

"How dreadful!" she murmured, with a consciousness of undreamed depths in herself. "Of course he is the only one — the only one!" and across the water she begged his forgiveness.

But through all her agony of doubt in the days that followed, one shame was miraculously removed, one hope sang faintly beneath : she, too, had her power ! A glance in the street had called her from one army of her sisters to the other, and the difference was inestimable.

Her classes stared at her with naïve admiration. The girls in the house begged for her as a chaperon to Amherst entertainments, and sulked when a report that the young hosts found her too attractive to enable strangers to distinguish readily between her and her charges rendered another selection advisable. The fact that her interest in them was fitful, sometimes making her merry and intimate, sometimes relegating them to a connection purely professional, only left her more interesting to them ; and boxes of flowers, respectful solicitations to spreads, and tempting invitations to long drives through the lengthening afternoons began to elect her to an obvious popularity. Once it would have meant much to her ; she marvelled now at the little shade of jealousy with which her colleagues assured her of it. How long must she wait? When would life be real again?

She seemed to herself to move in a dream that heightened and strained quicker as it neared an inevitable shock of waking — to what? Even at the best, to what? Even supposing that — she put it boldly, as if it had been another woman — she should marry the man who had asked her seven years ago, what was there in the very obvious future thus assured her that could match the hopes her heart held out? How could it be at once the golden harbor, the peaceful end of hurried, empty years, and the delicious, shifting unrest that made a tumult of her days and nights? Yet something told her that it was; something repeated insistently, "Always I will wait." . . . He would keep faith, that grave, big man!

But every day, as she moved with tightened lips to the table where the mail lay spread, coloring at a foreign stamp, paling with the disappointment, her hope grew fainter. He dared not write and tell her. It was over. Violet shadows darkened her eyes; a feverish flush made her, as it grew and faded at the slightest warning, more girlish than ever.

But the young life about her seemed only to mock her own late weakened impulse. It was not the same. She was playing heavy stakes: they hardly realized the game. All but one, they irritated her. This one, since her first short call, had come and come again. No explanations, no confidences, had passed between them; their sympathy, deep-rooted, expressed itself perfectly in the ordinary conventional tone of two reserved if congenial natures. The girl did not discuss herself, the woman dared not. They talked of books, music, travel; never, as if by tacit agreement, of any of the countless possible personalities in a place so given to personal discussion.

She could not have told how she knew that the girl had come to college to please a mother whose great regret was to have missed such training, nor did she remember when her incurious friend had learned her tense determination of flight; she could have sworn that she had never spoken of it. Sometimes, so perfectly did they appear to understand each other beneath an indifferent conversation, it seemed to her that the words must be the merest symbols, and that the girl who always caught her lightest shade of meaning knew to exactness her alternate hope and fear, the rudderless tossing toward and from her taunting harbor-light.

They sat by an open window, breathing in the moist air from the fresh, upturned earth. The gardeners were working over the sprouting beds; the sun came in warm and sweet.

"Three weeks ago it was almost cold at this time," said the girl. "In the springtime I give up going home, and

love the place.   But two years more —
two years ! ”

“ Do you really mind it so much ? ”

“ I think what I mind the most is that
I don’t like it more,” said the girl slowly.
“ Mamma wanted it so.   She really loved
study.   I don’t, but if I did — I should
love it more than this.   This would seem
so childish.   And if I just wanted a good
time, why, then this would seem such a
lot of trouble.   All the good things here
seem — seem remedies ! ”

The older woman laughed nervously.
Three weeks — three weeks and no word!

“ You will be making epigrams, my
dear, if you don’t take care,” she said
lightly.   “ But you’re going to finish just
the same ?   The girls like you, your work
is good ; you ought to stay.”

The girl flashed a look of surprise at
her.   It was her only hint of sympathy.

“ You advise me to ? ” she asked
quietly.

“ I think it would be a pity to disappoint your mother," with a light hand on her shoulder. "You are so young — four years is very little. Of course you could do the work in half the time, but you admit that you are not an ardent student. If nobody came here but the girls that really needed to, we shouldn't have the reputation that we have. The girls to whom this place means the last word in learning and the last grace of social life are estimable young women, but not so pleasant to meet as you."

Three weeks — but he had waited seven years !

"I am very childish," said the girl. "Of course I will stay. And some of it I like very much. It's only that mamma doesn't understand. She overestimates it so. Somehow, the more complete it is, the more like everything else, the more you have to find fault with on all sides. I'd rather have come when mamma was a girl."

"I see. I have thought that, too."

Ah, fool, give up your senseless hope! You had your chance — you lost it. Fate cannot stop and wait while you grow wise.

" When that shadow covers the hill, I will give it up forever. Then I will write to Henry's wife and ask her to let me come and help take care of the children. She will like it, and I can get tutoring if I want it. I will make the children love me, and there will be a place where I shall be wanted and can help," she thought.

The shadow slipped lower. The fresh turf steeped in the last rays, the birds sang, the warming earth seemed to have touched the very core of spring. Her hopes had answered the eager year, but her miracle was too wonderful to be.

A light knock at the door, and a maid came toward her, tray in hand. She lifted the card carelessly — her heart dropped a moment and beat in hard, slow throbs. Her eyes filled with tears; her cheeks were hot and brilliant.

“ I will be there in a moment.”   How deep her voice sounded !

The girl slipped by her.

“ I was going anyway,” she said softly. “ Good-by !   Don’t touch your hair — it’s just right.”

She did not wait for an answer, but went out.   As she passed by the little reception-room a tall, eager man made toward her with outstretched hands.   Her voice trembled as she laughed.

“ No, no — I’m not the one,” she murmured, “ but she — she’s coming ! ”

A HOPE DEFERRED

A HOPE DEFERRED

MISS SABINA dropped a lump of sugar into each of the little cups and poured the coffee with a pretty carefulness, handing one across the table and rising with a grace that was almost girlish.

"Shall we drink it on the porch?" she asked, in her gentle, deprecating voice with the minor tone in it, that one associated with her as closely as her gray dress, her quaint old-fashioned rings, and the faint odor of dried rose-leaves — not attar or essence of rose, but dried rose-leaves — that went with her when she walked.

For ten years she had asked this question, pleasantly, deferentially ; and for ten years M. Laroche had taken his cup, preceded her to the door that opened directly on the piazza, bowed low as he held it for her to pass, and exclaimed with an ever-fresh enthusiasm, " Ze porrch, by all means ! "

It was a pleasant porch with a climbing vine and a box of scarlet geraniums, and directly in front of it a little unfenced green with a small fountain — the park of the street, which was one of those clean and faded byways of a rapidly growing city that surprise the discoverer with a sense of what the old town used to be two generations ago. The rumble of the city died away before one entered Maple Avenue ; the women sat and gossiped on the stoops ; the children played happily in the park ; the late afternoon seemed almost rural as the sun slanted through the maples that shaded either side of the narrow, dusty road.

Miss Sabina finished her coffee and

wiped her fingers daintily. In the fading glow her pale hair turned almost golden, and her soft cheeks took a deeper tint — one realized what a charmingly pretty girl she must have been. She looked long at the green before them and broke the friendly silence:

" How well the grass is looking, monsieur, for this time of year ! "

M. Laroche beamed expressively on the grass. " But how charming, Mlle. Sabine, and how green ! It is also neat — so neat ! "

Miss Sabina sighed.

" I suppose that in England it is much, much finer," she said softly. " I suppose we haven't the least idea of the parks there — one must see them."

M. Laroche shrugged his shoulders.

" Ah, ze parrks ! *C'est possible* — it may be. But zey are damp, verry damp — *n'est-ce pas ?* "

Miss Sabina smiled gently to herself, with eyes that saw beyond the little green.

"And the abbeys, monsieur! Westminster and Oxford and Melrose! Only think of standing — of *my* standing — by Melrose Abbey!"

M. Laroche raised his brows eloquently and appeared lost in contemplation of the picture.

"Ah, yes! Indeed!" he sighed. "Zat is a great abbey — Mel-h-rose!"

"And London, monsieur, and the Tower! And Fleet Street, and Piccadilly, and the Strand! How strange it is to feel that you know them so well, that you love them so well, and yet that you've never seen them. When we used to play, my cousins and I, in Grandfather Endicott's house, and choose what pictures we would have, I always took 'Melrose Abbey from the South' and a big engraving of Windsor Castle. The children used to laugh at me, but I always chose them. Cousin Frank used to tease me and say that I'd never get there, and that girls couldn't travel around like boys. Grandmother Endicott, too, she was so cold and distant toward me; you see, she hated poor mother so. When Cousin Frank's will was read she was very, very angry. I don't know whether I told you that she said quite publicly that it was absurd for a woman of my age to be so crazy for travelling. I thought that rather unkind, for she's been so much herself. But then, she's so old, perhaps she's not quite responsible. She's eighty-four, you know."

"Ah," said M. Laroche, with admiration, "she is verry old, verry old indeed, your grandmozzer!"

He was as charmingly attentive, as gallantly interested, as if he had not heard it all before a hundred times over. Every movement of his expressive, whimsical face meant courteous regard; every attitude of his figure, a little bent now, in clothes a little shabby, but so exquisitely mended and brushed and polished that the necessity for such artistic care seemed almost fortunate, expressed close and deferential sympathy with the eager, vivid soul beside him.

And the interest might well have been unfeigned, for under those smooth gray folds beat a `vigorous, determined heart that forty years of denial and monotony could not still nor tame. The soft, calm eyes of this New England spinster had never looked beyond her native town; but in fancy she had voyaged the seas for years, and in her dreams she wandered through strange and wonderful streets of foreign lands and heard the speech of all the peoples of the world. No schoolboy was ever more thirsty for the ends of the earth than she; this little stay-at-home knew all the routes by sea and land, and delighted in the customs of the fortunate dwellers in the places of her lifelong desire.

To-night her hand shook as she laid the coffee-cup aside, and the flush in her cheeks did not die with the sunset. A twinge of remorse defied her tremulous joy; a nervous fear of her unworthiness came over her, and it was with an uncertain voice that she approached her friend.

"It seems as if I were almost too old, monsieur. Perhaps some younger person ought to have it, after all. I've gone on so long without it —

"I asked Mr. Alden about it last Sunday, after morning service. I said it seemed dreadful to be so perfectly happy, and Cousin Frank just dead! But how can I help it? Frank knew just how I'd feel. It's just as he said: 'When I go to heaven, Sabina shall go to Europe, if she's alive, and I don't know which of us'ill be the happier.' And then to think of Miss Ellsworth and her friends going, and wanting me to go with them — it seemed too good to be true! I asked Mr. Alden if he thought Grandmother Endicott ought to have said the will was blasphemous, and he said no, that it was a nice will and a kind one. And I nearly cried right there. I could just get out, 'Oh, Mr. Alden, you don't know what this means to me — you don't know!' and then I had to run right away, or I'd have broken down."

M. Laroche nodded sympathetically. "Zat is a good man, M. Aldenne, *très aimable* — most kind. I sink every one likes heem. It is but yesterday zat he has asked me, 'And where do you go when Mees Sabina is away, monsieur? You will not find anozzer soch landlady, *hein?* I sink not.' He is a kind man."

"Miss Ellsworth wanted me to take some German lessons, and there was a 'Life of Goethe' she wanted me to read. But I couldn't do that. The time's so short now. And I'm too old to go to school again. So I just had to tell her then and there.

"'Miss Ellsworth,' I said, 'it isn't quite the same with me as 'tis with you. You've been before and you know all the places from experience, not just as I do from books, so I'm glad to go with you. But I must tell you, Miss Ellsworth, that I'm not going to learn, the way you are. I'm just going for pleasure and happiness and comfort, and nothing else. You know how it is with me. All my life I've had to stay right here, and I could only live decently and as father would have wanted me to live — we're Endicotts, you know, if we are the poor branch — by scrimping and saving and being very, very careful, and making things last. Almost the last thing poor father said to me was to keep things up.

"'"There's just enough, Sabina, if you're careful, to do it," he said. "I want you should always have the house neat, and a good, plain, nice little dinner with the silver, and a cup of coffee after, and a bottle of wine kept, in case mother should ever come in. And the engravings and the pianoforte and those mahogany things, and the mother-o'-pearl cabinet — never let 'em go, Sabina.   When they come in to our funerals I don't want anybody to be ashamed of the Endicotts — it's a gentleman's house."

"'So I've kept everything up,' I said, 'though many's the time I'd have given the world to let Hannah go, and do for myself, and sell the things, and just get to Europe, and tramp through it, if I had to, like those two teachers from your school.   But of course 'twould have been ridiculous — a woman of my age! And I didn't dare take the money for the funeral and if sickness should come, and go with that, for it would break father's heart — he had it all planned out. And of course a woman doesn't need to go — 'tisn't as if I were a man —'"

M. Laroche pursed his lips and shook his head thoughtfully.

"But if zat is ze sing you want, what deeference is it zat you are not a man?" he asked luminously.

Miss Sabina threw him a grateful glance.

"'So you see, Miss Ellsworth,' I said, 'here's my chance. Now, I don't care if I don't understand them in Paris or Berlin. I can see them, I can hear them, I can walk on the sidewalks and breathe the air, can't I? I can see the shops and the houses and the palaces and the canals, and how the sky looks there. I can go from one country to another, and be on the ocean, and perhaps I can see the Alps. I don't need to know French and German to appreciate them, do I? I want to just go and drink it in and realize that it's really I — that I'm there. There's only ten weeks or so, and then I'll come home, but I'll live on it all the rest of my life!' Oh, monsieur, what will I care that I haven't any money then?'"

Her eyes were glowing, her breath came fast; she was home again, in fancy, with her precious load of memories and experiences, and down on her knees before the treasures that were to adorn her henceforth quiet life.

M. Laroche looked at her with admiration.

"*Ma'm'selle, vous êtes grande dame, vous,*" he said, wondering at the pink flush and the thrown-back head.

She sank back, ashamed of such a display of feeling.

"I run on like a chatterbox of a girl," she said shyly. "You'll think I'm a self-ish, talkative old thing, monsieur."

He bowed gallantly.

"Zat would never be, Mlle. Sabine," he said. "And your affairs, are zey not mine? But yes! Indeed!"

They sat quietly for a time, in the dusk, watching the evening star grow before them, enjoying the cool stillness and the scent of the freshly watered green. The young people strolling by now and then smiled at them for a contented pair of middle-aged friends, and thought their pleasant quiet the placid repose of those who have tacitly done with life and its strong tides of feeling.

They could not know that the woman with the softly parted hair was all a-tremble for romance, thirsty for adventure, bohemian-souled and utterly fearless; they could not see the heart of the little foreigner with the shabby clothes and gray imperial, how it was eaten up with homesickness and regret — with all his gratitude to his gentle hostess — for France, with her queen city, her familiar sights and smells, her zest and color, and more than all, the fishing-coast where his mother had rocked him to sleep in sight of the sails.

They sighed together, and blushed, and glanced quickly aside, and Miss Sabina rose hastily and slipped through the long French window.

"Shall I sing?" she asked, not waiting for an answer to a question of such long usage. While she felt through the dusk to the old pianoforte, M. Laroche lit his cigarette and waited with gentle expectation. The lilacs from the next yard drifted in and met the faint odor from the old china rose-jar that stood on the polished mahogany table inside. The first few notes of the piano carried with them to him who knew the room so well a never-fading picture of the peaceful, old-time parlor: the willow plates in the mother-o'-pearl cabinet, the "Sistine Madonna" and Correggio's "Holy Night," the dim oil-paintings that great-grandmother Endicott had made so long ago, the bronze Chinese idol that squatted near the rose-jar, the dusky, elusive pierglass with its dull gilding of another generation and its mysterious, haunting reflections — they were all confused with the tune that Miss Sabina's sweet, reedy voice had so often quavered through; a tune that she would not have known by its title of "Fair Harvard":

Believe me, if all those endearing young charms,
   That I gaze on so fondly to-day,
Were to change by to-morrow and to fleet
     in my arms,
   Like fairy gifts fading away,

Thou wouldst still be adored as this moment
    thou art,
  Let thy loveliness fade as it will,
And around the dear ruin each wish of my
    heart
  Would entwine itself verdantly still.

Miss Sabina knew other songs —
"When other lips and other hearts,"
and "Joys that we've tasted," and
"Come with thy lute to the fountain";
but into this one she threw most mar-
vellously all the passion of her yet girlish, tender heart; and the yellow keys
yielded to her tremulous touch a throb-
bing, jarring melody that came to the
listener like an old perfume from some
dusty, just found rose-jar of a long-
dead beauty.

It is not while beauty and youth are thine own,
  And thy cheeks unprofaned by a tear,
That the fervor and faith of a soul can be
    known,
  To which time will but make thee more
    dear.

M. Laroche smiled.

" 'And zy chicks onprofenned by a tearr,' " he repeated softly. "Ah, yes! Indeed ! "

No ; the heart that has truly lov'd never
    forgets,
  But as truly loves on to the close,
As the sunflower turns on her god, when he
    sets,
  The same look which she turn'd when he
    rose.

The last faint quaver died away, there was a light rustle of skirts, and Miss Sabina stood at the window.

"Good night, monsieur," she said softly.

M. Laroche tossed away the end of his cigarette.

"*Vous chantez très bien, mademoiselle,*" he said, with his inimitable bow. "Good night."

And with this, his invariable phrase, he went to his room off the piazza.

Miss Sabina had been waiting a long time when he came to breakfast the next morning, heavy-eyed from a night which he admitted to have been sleepless, and too tired to present his apologies with the whimsical grace that gave his simplest words and acts such a kindly flavor. His hostess watched his untouched plate with concern, and suddenly cut short her small, friendly confidences of ways and means for the summer, struck by his languid manner and weary eyes.

"Why, monsieur, you're eating nothing! Is it the headache again? You surely won't go out to-day and try to teach — it's too much!"

He tried to rally, and smiled bravely at her anxious eyes, made his little negative gesture that was half gratitude to the questioner, and would have turned the talk; but Miss Sabina was alarmed in earnest. The thought that he might be alone and sick in the summer cut sharply for a second, and her quick fancy saw

him in the agony of his terrible headaches, housed with strangers, lonely and
too proud to ask for help. Her eyes
filled with tears, and she leaned impul-
sively across the table.

"Oh, monsieur, you're ill — you're
really ill!" she cried. "Go to the doctor — promise me you'll go! You've
not been the same for a week, now;
you've been so tired and worn. I've
noticed it ever since last week. It was
when I first got the notice from Cousin
Frank's lawyer that the money was in the
bank that you had that terrible headache;
don't you know how we sat and talked
till so late, and I was so excited? And
I've been talking so much and planning
so hard that I haven't thought — oh, I'm
very selfish, monsieur! It's terrible to
think of you being sick just when I'm
so happy. You'll go to the doctor?
Promise me you will!"

He shook his head.

"But zere is no need for a doctorre,

Mlle. Sabine, indeed no ! It is only to-day — I am well to-morrow. Not to sleep, it makes one weary for the day — *n'est-ce pas?* It is not a good country ·for sleep, I have found. In France I have always slept, ah, most easily ! But here, no. In France — "

He paused a moment, and the room was perfectly still. He looked at her, but he did not see her, and Miss Sabina had a strange, swift memory of her little brother who died at school, and the look in his eyes when he cried to be taken home.

It was over in a moment, and M. Laroche shrugged his shoulders lightly.

"One imagines I come to America to sleep, *hein?*" he asked her, with such a humorous, friendly smile that she half forgot her anxiety. But before he left for the old school, where dwindling classes lessened his scanty salary every year, she had made him promise to see the doctor before night.

" And a cup of tea with your lunch—
don't forget, monsieur!" she called after
him as he walked off—she hated to realize how slowly, nowadays. They were
good friends, these two, and they knew
it well : if she came back and he was not
there — her heart contracted and seemed
to wait while she caught her breath and
shook the thought away.

" We're not so old as that," she whispered under her breath. " We're not
really old, either of us !"

All day she thought about him, and to
her just quickened sight much that the
excitement of the past had made trivial
loomed suddenly large before her. She
realized how quiet he had grown of late,
how seldom he essayed the jokes, the small
kindly nonsense, the half-serious homage
to her charm of personality that brightened her life so much — that had been,
indeed, almost her only social pleasure.
It occurred to her that he had been less
quick of comprehension than ever before,

less ready to follow her mood with that wonderful delicacy of perception that had enabled her—shy, secluded, half troubled at the restlessness of her own eager heart —to talk to him as she had never been able to talk to her only sister. She remembered how every innocent ruse for concealing the scantiness of a meal had succeeded of late, and how unconsciously he had, at any excuse of hers, eaten what he would once have indignantly insisted that she should share. But more than all this, he had talked as he had never talked before of his childhood and his childhood's home. Miss Sabina had learned her Paris well from him long ago. For years in the winter evenings, when they could not enjoy the piazza and the green, they had sat by the Franklin grate in the sitting-room, and she had followed him breathlessly through " Les Misérables " — his rapid and broken translation heightening incalculably the sense of strangeness and intensity — or

he had led her about Paris and its out-
skirts till she had grown to an actual
intimacy with that city of his dreams ; for
hitherto it had been Paris that he had
spoken of as his home, where he had
lived since he was a boy of ten with his
older brother Jules, who had written a
" French Grammar for Beginners " and
was enrolled by M. Laroche among the
great lights of his native literature.

But of late when he spoke of France
it was to no city that he carried his eager
listener, but to a little fishing-village,
with the nets drying on the sand, and the
setting sun on the sails, and the clatter of
his white-capped mother's sabots as she
led him down to the beach to kiss his
sunburnt father. The rush and clamor
of the city streets died away before the
sleepy Breton cradle-song, and the lights
of the boulevard faded as he watched the
stars shine down upon the sea in that
land so far from him.

Miss Sabina thought how her father

toward the end had told her over and over of the games at school and the holi-days at the old Endicott home, and had even described the old play-room to her, as if his mother had never ceased to love him and mend his broken toys. Did men always remember, then, at the end? Did it mean — but she threw it off again and told herself, "We're not so old as that! We're not really *old!*"

At dinner that night she would have talked of nothing but his health and her fears for his lonely summer, but he would have none of that.

"I do quite well, you shall see, *chère mademoiselle;* I greet you in ze *autom'* at ze — ze docke. You are surprise', you do not know me — I am so restored! *Est-ce possible! ce pauv' Laroche! Comme il se porte bien*—how he is well!"

His expressive pantomime, his laugh, his old kindly smile as he met her eyes, frankly, yet with that confidential regard that seemed to say more than his words, almost deceived her; but even as she laughed, his lids drooped, his smile faded, and he fingered the cloth restlessly under her steady gaze.

"I don't know, monsieur, I don't know," she said, in her soft, troubled minor voice. "You weren't so well this last fall, you know; the heat wore on you dreadfully. I wish you could go away somewhere and rest this summer, and not take those vacation classes — I wish you would!"

He shook his head. "R-h-est? R-h-est?" he said softly to himself, and with the throaty little *r* that was so marked when he was absent-minded. "In zis country? *Jamais, jamais, mademoiselle.* It is queeck, queeck! *immédiatement* — at once! Teach me zis moment — it is no matter zat it takes you a lifetime to learn — teach me zis moment—I mus' know it zis verry day! I mus' run now to somesing else, but I come ag-gain, and you teach me immediately ag-gain, for I have forgotten it all. But zere is no time to lose—no, indeed!"

She was amazed at the bitterness of his tone; she could hardly understand, he poured out the words so quickly, but she could see that this was more than a passing irritation, that his years of teaching were beginning to tell on him. Before she could reply he had risen and opened the door, and she found herself passing through to the porch without the formula of invitation that preceded the coffee. When he joined her with the neglected cups the storm had passed, and as he talked quietly of the preparation for the voyage that had formed the subject of their evening conversation for weeks, she could hardly realize the depths of weariness and loathing that the sudden glimpse of exhausted patience had shown her.

That night Miss Sabina did not sing. She played through two or three of the stiff, sweet little preludes, but the lilacs were so strong, the old melodies waked such confused, excited sadness in her, that the songs would not come. The sight of that keen, drooping profile dark against the orange glow reproached her somehow with its loneliness—how many weeks he would sit alone!—and she rose hastily and went out again.

"You do not sing? You have not ze mood, *hein? Eh bien*, not to sing, it is well sometimes." . . . And they sat in silence long after the stars came out.

That night Miss Sabina slept lightly. Strange, confused dreams, half-conscious delusions, troubled her with voices that she knew were unreal, that yet murmured and muttered and droned, till, in her effort to dismiss them and sink to deeper sleep, she woke with a start. Surely some one was talking! She hesitated, and from somewhere below her came the sound of a voice that rose and fell almost monotonously — not loud, but clear and continuous. Without a moment's hesitation she got out of bed, put on a dressing-gown and slippers, and opening her door quietly, paused a moment at the head of the stairs before going down. Without doubt it was a voice, and only one. The fear that a more timid woman would have felt in the first uncertainty of waking came to her now with the conviction that this was no thief, no stranger, but her ten years' friend, speaking with a passionate earnestness that terrified her; appealing — to whom? — with a sadness, a despair, that wrung her heart.

She slipped like a shadow down the stair, and crouching on the lowest step, she listened breathlessly for a moment. Ah, yes! It was to her he was talking! Her own name, in his strange, sweet, French handling of it, came to her through the half-open door. She looked through the warped and widened crack at the side, where the light streamed through, unconscious of the time, the place, even of her silent, peering attitude, knowing only that a deep, ominous excitement thrilled her to the very centre of her soul.

He had sunk exhausted on the narrow white bed, a thin, pathetic figure in a faded, mended silk dressing-gown, with a tired white face and black eyes that glowed like coals. His hands were clinched between his knees, his head hung upon his breast. His voice was weak and strained now, no longer the deep tone that had waked her, and his quaint broken English, as if he saw her there before him, was sadder than any eloquence.

"'But you will go to ze doctorre — promise me you will go.' Ah, *mon Dieu*, Mlle. Sabine, what good is zat? I want no doctorre — me; I want my home! To you, what is it? But only a strange land, a new people, a voyage, and you come back. Ah, me, I am twelve years away! Twelve years away!

"'You work too hard, you need rest'

I tell heem I must work ; I come here to work — would I rest here ?

"'You must go back to France, you fret yourself too much ; you have ze weak heart, monsieur, you are here too long already.' *Dame!* Is it zat I stay for my pleasure ?

"'I have no medicine for you, monsieur; it is not ze doctorre nor ze tonique nor ze r-h-est for you — it is to go home. Ze systemme it runs down, down, zen ze heart it grows weak, weak, and zen, monsieur, *vous savez*, it stops.' . . .

"'*Mais*, monsieur, I cannot go, I have not ze money — ze school grows small, I am so often sick.' Ah, mademoiselle, figure to yourself ! I, Sylvestre Laroche, say zis to a stranger — I speak so !

"'It is to regret, monsieur. Zere is no friend — ?'

"'Monsieur, I have no money but a little ; how shall I pay ?'

"Ah, Mlle. Sabine, how can I laugh

wiz you? How shall I stay alone? But how can I go? I know so few. I say, 'Lend me money so zat I go home,' and zey say to me, '*Mon Dieu*, M. Laroche, how do you pay zis money? To-morrow? Next year?' I do not know. I cannot tell zem. . . .

"'And if I go, monsieur, I am well? I need fear no more ze heart?' 'Ah, monsieur, who can tell? Maybe yes, maybe no. It is to guard well against ze worry, ze alarrm, ze queeck starrt — *vous savez?* Ten years, five years, one year — I cannot tell, monsieur.'

"*C'est terrible, n'est-ce pas, Mlle. Sabine? Vous partez demain.* You are so soon gone, and I stay here! And I am twelve years away from home — and I have ze weak heart. *Vous me dites 'au revoir,' mademoiselle — moi, je vous dis 'adieu.'*"

The woman crouching on the stair bit her lip and pressed her finger-nails into her hands to keep back the sobs that shook her. It seemed to her that he must hear the beating of her heart, that every long, hard breath would surely startle him. So helpless, so poor, so horribly, hopelessly sad! She had read of terrible homesickness — the Swiss for his Alps, the peasant for his farm; they seemed romantic, elemental, vague. But this little Frenchman, this dapper chatterer of the light-heartedest language in all the world, did he harbor this tragedy? For to her tender, unworn heart the tragedy was remorselessly clear. This bent figure in its faded dressing-gown; this face almost strange to her in its worn, gray anguish; these nerveless, half-open hands — she read them all too well.

"Oh, no, he mustn't, he mustn't!" she whispered, and grasped the banisters, and tried to turn away her eyes: for his own filled slowly before her.

She got up the stairs, her fingers in her ears, stumbling over the long wrapper, seeming to herself to wake the house

with every misstep.   She closed her eyes
not to see that strained, white face, and
saw it plainer in the dark.   Her thoughts
were all a confused pain, an incoherent
revolt at the cruelty of it, the help-
lessness ; for what could she do ?   Even
she, who cared for him so — ah, how she
cared ! — what could she —

Her hand jumped to her heart and
clutched rigidly there ; her breath went,
and she gasped like the drowning man
under the last sucking breaker ; her
strength left in a great sickening ebb, and
she grasped the bedpost with all her
might.

"No, no !   Oh, no, no !" she cried
weakly.   "Oh, no !"   She felt her way
to the bed and dropped on it, utterly unconscious that she had moved since that
wave of desolation broke on her.   She
seemed to have been standing by the
bedpost, grasping it hard and thinking
there, for years.

She saw him as he had come to her

so long ago : handsome, polite, younger then, and merrier perhaps, with his inimitable bow and the neat printed card :

M. Sylvestre Laroche,
Paris.
Irregular Verbs a Specialty.
Conversation Classes Formed.

How she had admired him! She had felt sure that father would never have objected to his lodging there, recommended by Mr. Alden, too! How amusing he had been, how constantly cheerful; how exquisitely sympathetic when her sister died! She could not send him away then.

He had been so gentle, so thoughtful, so interested in all her small affairs, so forgetful of his own. How grateful he was for the slightest attendance when his terrible headaches weakened him for days, and how charmingly he had thanked her for what she had done! Hardly a day during that long winter sickness, when she would have died if left alone to her nervous melancholy, that he did not bring home some flower or bit of fruit. She guessed later what meagre lunches had made their purchase possible. One of his pupils would have taken him South for the winter vacation, but he had refused and stayed with her. And the cold tried him so.

"I shall never forget this, monsieur," she had said, when she found it out; she had not thought to be able to repay that quiet sacrifice.

How sweetly, how sympathetically he had listened to her plans; how he had helped, suggested, advised, admired, and congratulated! The very pattern of her travelling-dress, the marking of her trunk — and he sick for home, dying in a foreign land!

"*C'est terrible, n'est-ce pas, Mlle. Sabine?*"

What was it, that strange pain that

never ceased, that hopeful, hopeless yearning? She had never left her home or country ; she knew only the happy dream of one day seeing another, not her own, fair, strange, and distant; she was homesick for new lands. Did he feel what she felt — did he feel perhaps more? Her heart cried out that this could not be, but she hushed it, and saw him growing slowly old, old, waiting for the lurking death —how soon would it come? a year, a month? — dreaming of France and youth, waking to the dull reality ; sitting alone in a strange, cheap boarding-house, while she went gayly from land to land.

"*Vous me dites ' au revoir,' mademoiselle — moi, je vous dis ' adieu.'*"

She knew little French, but she understood that, and as that harsh sob rang in her ears again, as she saw that bent figure, that hopeless face, she knew in one quick, far-seeing flash of bereavement that it was over, that she could bear her

own sorrow, but not his; she could stay
—she could not let him. Waves of
pain broke against her resolution, tug-
ging remonstrance, momentary weakness,
passionate prayers to make this happiness
possible for both of them, but beneath it
all was the certainty: it was done.

She met him at breakfast with a nervous flush that hid the pallor of the
night, with a voice whose cheerfulness
amazed her, with an excitement she had
never thought to feel again. He was
gaunt and hollow-eyed, and yielded readily to her persuasions to stay at home,
rousing himself to assure her that he
would allow this small indulgence only
because she was going so soon.

"It is but four—five days now, and
you are gone, Mlle. Sabine, and zen I
shall not want ze vacation, *hein?* So I
stay. I have but one class only, and I
sink I do not teach it well to-day," he
said, with elaborate cheerfulness. She

poured the coffee and drank a little of her own.

"I'm not so sure I shall be gone in four or five days, monsieur," she returned easily.

He stared vaguely at her. "No? You wait for some one take ze place of M. Ellsworse?"

She drew a long breath and clasped her hands beneath the table.

"Monsieur," she said, with an almost humorous smile, "I suppose you'll think I'm a very silly woman, but I can't help it — I've about decided I'm not going at all."

"*Mais, mademoiselle, qu' avez-vous donc?* What is zis zat you say? *Mon Dieu!*"

She shook her head.

"You see, I've lived here now more than forty years, and when I came to think of leaving Hannah and the house and father's things — and the house isn't insured — and when I remembered how Miss Ellsworth is seasick —"

"*Mais, Mlle. Sabine, ce n'est pas possible*; zis is in fon zat you talk——"

"Indeed, it is not, monsieur; I'm in earnest. You see, I'm at home"—her voice fell, and she paused a moment—"I'm quite safe here. If I should get sick in—in England, who'd take care of me? It is not as if I were young and strong; it is not as if Miss Ellsworth was to be with me always. And I can't speak French or German, and—and all these steamer accidents frighten me terribly! I just lie awake nights imagining——"

"*Mais, mais, Mlle. Sabine*——"

His startled, tired face was too much for her: he was too exhausted to adjust himself to this sudden turn, and some instinct warned her to go straight ahead and say it all, before he had time to notice her dark-ringed eyes and nervous, broken voice.

"Don't you see, monsieur, what I'm trying to say?" she asked quickly.

"Don't you see that we've both been planning wrong? that it's I who ought to stay, and you who ought to go? No, no; let me finish! Here am I, a fussy old maid, born and brought up here all my life, silly enough to imagine I could ever really like it away from home. Why, monsieur, do *you* like it away from home? And here are you, who want a vacation, who'd like to see your friends and your family, who'd thoroughly enjoy every minute of it. It's you who can take Mr. Ellsworth's berth, dear monsieur! We're such old friends, you and I—"

"Mlle. Sabine! I take your money, *par exemple!* I go—*ah, jamais de la vie! C'est impossible*—"

He dropped his head upon his arms, and she leaned over him, stroking his hair, holding his hands, her timidity utterly gone, her heart carried away and exalted above all girlishness in the magnitude of her love and sacrifice. For this hour he was hers—her child to comfort, her brother to help, her lover, for whom any offering was too small. She was no longer the ignorant, untravelled little spinster: she had flung away all her own hopes and fears to be the life and happiness of one poor soul that had none but her, and at that height the world seems small indeed.

"*Mais*, mademoiselle, I take your money and go home, I restore myself, I return — how do I pay? I sink till now zat you desire to go more zan to do anysing — I say nossing zen. Now zat you fear to go, you want your home (ah, Mlle. Sabine, *vous avez raison :* to be home, *c'est le paradis!*), now I tell you zat, I, too, I die if I go not back to France! I am too long away. . . . But how do I pay? I pay someway, *vous savez*, I will not go else!"

"But, monsieur, you will get it when you get there! Don't you remember your brother's book — the Grammar? You always said that if ever you got to

France you could make them give you that share. It's yours, monsieur: you ought to have it!"

His face flushed; he seized her hands and clutched them till she could have screamed with the pain. He babbled incoherent thanks and blessings. He saw himself returned with double her loan. His delight was childish to think that he should have forgotten *that*! And when, struck by sudden misgiving, he let go her hands:

"Ah, mademoiselle, it is long ago, all zat! It is mine, yes; but if I cannot get it? *Ce n'est pas sûr, ça* — I cannot tell if I shall have from all zat one single sou — "

"Monsieur," she said, with sincerity and pride, "I have been poor all my life. You would have done this for me, I am sure — you did something just like it once. Will you not let me give as I should like to for once in my life? I believe you will pay it back: if you can't, are you too proud to please an old friend ?"

He took her hand again and kissed it. "*Vous êtes tout à fait grande dame, mademoiselle*," he said simply. "*Vous me sauvez la vie.* I will go."

After that the days were hours to her, the hours minutes. She tasted the full sweet of her renunciation, she rode on the top wave of the strange, excited joy that urged her on to the minutest preparations for his comfort. He moved in a waking dream, a confused tremble of happiness; he could not know her alternations of fierce regret and quiet resignation, he did not see how the hand shook that filled his plate, nor how the eyes that smiled so kindly and serenely into his were red with crying. *Le bon Dieu* had laid in his lap the blessing he was hungering and thirsting after, and he took it with the happy blindness of a starving child.

The days flew in preparations. He was utterly helpless with delight, and while she packed and mended and brought out in a very luxury of giving the little conveniences of travel that had pleased her so in that far-away last week, he sang his old French songs, and kissed her hand, and was a boy again in the home he was to see so soon.

Only when she laid a certain embroidered case in the trunk, filled with tiny pockets whose uses she had once so delightedly explained to him, did her expression vaguely trouble him.

"You are sad, Mlle. Sabine! You would go? You change ze mind—" But she smiled at him and said that she was selfish enough to want him to stay, now that he was going so soon.

But he would soon be back; he would be with her in ten weeks!

The last day was gone, the last evening; the last breakfast lay untouched before them: she could do no more for him now. His carriage was at the door; then would come the train, then the noisy seaport city, then the wonderful great boat — he would be half the world away. Their hearts were too full for speech. This old Frenchman with his jaunty air, his shining boots, his mended gloves, this quiet, middle-aged woman with the pale, lined face, were not romantic to look upon; but one was struggling with a passionate gratitude that choked him, and the other was sending away from her — perhaps forever — the love and youth and brightness of her life.

The driver called; they loosed hands. He walked silently down the steps, but with an inarticulate cry she summoned him back. She put her arms around him, as about a child she would send away to school, and laid her cheek softly against his. He caught in her eyes what sent his hand to his heart.

"Mlle. Sabine! What is it you have

done? You would go — *mon Dieu*, you have lied to me!"

With one last effort she smiled away his sudden fear.

"Why, no!" she said through her tears. "Why, no, monsieur! I only miss my friend! Good-by!" And then, to please him, "*Bon voyage, mon ami!*"

When the carriage was out of sight she went in and cried by the old pianoforte — but not all for sorrow.

"He may come! He may come!" she sobbed over the yellow keys, and the old sounding-board thrilled softly and called back to her with a jangling minor cadence.

Her sobbing quieted to a sigh; beneath her tears her cheeks burned with a soft hot flush. "Maybe he will! Maybe he will!" she whispered, and "I know he will if he can!" while her hands clasped each other tightly, with fingers intertwisted like a girl's. She sat there

in the morning sunlight that turned her
hair to yellow, lost in strange, vague
dreams ; a shy happiness curved her lips
even while the new haunting pain that
tugged at her heart brought a tiny
wrinkle between her slender eyebrows.
She went about her simple household
duties half unconsciously. The old servant watched her curiously. She could
not understand why her mistress should
wipe her eyes, if later she could sing till
the dim parlor thrilled to the sweet old
tunes. Nor did Miss Sabina herself
quite certainly know. She was of a simple, modest generation that analyzed little: the rose of her life she could shut
away forever, hidden in some precious
yellowed book, but she could not tear
apart the leaves, even to know it better.

To Miss Ellsworth, who came in
later, hurried and amazed, she was inexplicable. She had travelled much, this
successful, ordinary woman, and she was
well educated, as women count such mat-
ters to-day ; but this quiet spinster, sit-

ting out of the strong currents of life, alone in her quaint, old-time parlor with its rose-leaves and mahogany of another day, had somehow left her behind with all her experiences and acquisitions, and bade her good-by with a manner that obliterated forever from her friend's mind the image of deprecating gentleness she had so long patronized.

For she had travelled the great way of all, had Miss Sabina, and the pride and happiness of her waiting heart had come to her in the steepest places of that wonderful road. The teacher of women since the beginning had spared no pains with this simple, eager soul, and she grew at once young and wise under the dear and unrelenting discipline.

"He will—he will if he can!" she whispered, as she waited for him on the porch, while the children played in the distance with faint, cheerful cries, and the roses grew strong toward dusk. And even to herself her tears seemed not wholly sad.

THE COURTING OF
LADY JANE

THE COURTING OF LADY JANE

THE colonel entered his sister's room abruptly, sat down on her bed, and scattered a drawerful of fluffy things laid out for packing.

"You don't seem to think about my side of the matter," he said gloomily. "What am I to do here all alone, for Heaven's sake?"

"That is so like a man," she murmured, one arm in a trunk. "Let me see: party-boots, the children's arctics, Dick's sweater — did you think I could live here forever, Cal?"

"Then you shouldn't have come at

all. Just as I get thoroughly settled down to flowers in the drawing-room, and rabbits in a chafing-dish, and people for dinner, you skip off. Why don't you bring the children here? What did you marry into the navy for, anyway? Nagasaki! I wouldn't live in a place called Nagasaki for all that money could buy!"

"You're cross," said Mrs. Dick placidly. "Please get off that bath-wrapper. If you don't like to live alone — Six bath-towels, Dick's shoe-bag, my old muff (I hope and pray I'll remember that!) Helen's reefer — Why don't you marry?"

"Marry? Marry! Are you out of your mind, Dosia? I marry!"

The colonel twisted his grayish mustache into points; a look of horror spread over his countenance.

"Men have done it," she replied seriously, "and lived. Look at Dick."

"Look at him? But how? Who

ever sees him? I've ceased to believe in him, personally. I can't look across the Pacific. Consider my age, Dosia; consider my pepper-and-salt hair; consider my bronchitis; consider — "

"Consider your stupidity! As to your hair, I should hate to eat a salad dressed with that proportion of pepper. As to your age, remember you're only ten years ahead of me, and I expect to remain thirty-eight for some time."

"But forty-eight is centenarian to a girl of twenty-two, Dosia."

The colonel was plaiting and un-plaiting the ball-fringe of the bed-slip; his eyes followed the motion of his fin-gers — he did not see his sister's trium-phant smile as she dived again into the trunk.

"That depends entirely on the girl. Take Louise Morris, for instance; she regards you as partly entombed, proba-bly " —the colonel winced involuntarily —"but, on the other hand, a girl like

Jane Leroy would have no such non-sense in her head, and she can't be much more than twenty."

"She is twenty-two," cried the unsuspecting colonel eagerly.

"Ah? I should not have said so much. Now such a girl as that, Ca!, handsome, dignified, college-bred, is just the wife for an older man. One can't seem to see her marrying some young snip of her own age. She'd be wasted on him. I happen to know that she refused Wilbur Vail entirely on that ground. She admitted that he was a charming fellow, but she told her mother he was far too young for her. And he was twenty-eight."

"Did she?" The colonel left the fringe. "But — but perhaps there were other reasons ; perhaps she didn't — "

"Oh, probably she didn't. But still, she said he was too young. That's the way with these serious girls. Now I thought Dick was middle-aged when I married him, and he was thirty. Jane doesn't take after her mother; she was only nineteen when she was born — I mean, of course, when Jane was born. Will you hand me that crocheted shawl, please?"

"My dear girl, you're not going to try to get that into that trunk, too? Something will break."

"Not at all, my dear Clarence. Thank you. Will you send Norah up to me as you go down?"

It had not occurred to the colonel that he was going down, but he decided that he must have been, and departed, forgetting Norah utterly before he had accomplished half of the staircase.

He wandered out through the broad hall, reaching down a hat absently, and across the piazza. Then, half unconscious of direction, he crossed the neat suburban road and strolled up the gravel path of the cottage opposite. Mrs. Leroy was sitting in the bay-window, attaching indefinite yards of white lace to indefinite yards of white ruffles. Jane, in cool violet lawn, was reading aloud to her. Both looked up at his light knock at the side door.

"But I am afraid I interrupt," he suggested politely, as he dropped into a low chair with a manner that betokened the assurance of a warm welcome.

"Not the least in the world," Mrs. Leroy smiled whimsically.

"Lady is reading Pater to me for the good of my soul, and I am listening politely for the good of her manners," she answered. "But it is a little wearing for us both, for she knows I don't understand it, and I know she thinks me a little dishonest for pretending to."

"Mother!"

The girl's gray eyes opened wide above her cool, creamy cheeks; the deep dimples that made her mother's face so girlish actually added a regularity and seriousness to the daughter's soft chin. Her chestnut hair was thick and straight, the little half-curls of the same rich tint that fell over her mother's forehead brushed wavelessly back on each side of a deep widow's peak.

The two older ones laughed.

"Always uncompromising, Lady Jane!" the colonel cried.

"I assure you, colonel, when Lady begins to mark iniquities, few of us stand!"

Jane smiled gravely, as on two children. "You know very well that is nonsense," she said.

Black Hannah appeared in the door, beaming and curtsying to the colonel.

"You-all ready foh yoh tea, Miss Lady?" she inquired.

A sudden recollection threw Mrs. Leroy into one of her irresistible fits of gentle laughter.

"Oh, Lady," she murmured, "do you remember that impossible creature that lectured me about Hannah's asking you for orders? Did I tell you about it, colonel?"

Jane shook her head reprovingly.

"Now, mother dearest, you always make him out worse—"

"Worse, my darling? Worse is a word that couldn't be applied to that man. Worse is comparative. Positive he certainly was, superlative is mild, but comparative—never!"

"Tell about it, do," begged the guest.

"Well, he came to see how Lady was growing up—he's a sort of species of relative—and he sat in your chair, colonel, and talked the most amazing Fourth Reader platitudes in a deep bass voice. And when Hannah asked Lady what her orders were for the grocer, he gave me a terrible look and rumbled out: 'I am grieved to see, Cousin Alice, that Jennie has burst her bounds!'

"It sounded horribly indecorous—I expected to see her in fragments on the floor—and I fairly gasped."

"Gasped, mother? You laughed in his face!"

"Did I, dearest? It is possible,"

Mrs. Leroy admitted. "And when I looked vague he explained, 'I mean that you seem to have relinquished the reins very early, Cousin Alice!'

"'Relinquished? Relinquished?' said I. 'Why, dear me, Mr. Wadham, I never held 'em!'"

"He only meant, mother dear, that—"

"Bless you, my child, I know what he only meant! He explained it to me very fully. He meant that when a widow is left with a ten-year-old child, she should apply to distant cousins to manage her and her funds."

"Disgusting beast!" the colonel exclaimed with feeling, possessing himself of one of Hannah's beaten biscuits, and smiling as Lady Jane's white fingers dropped just the right number of lumps in his tea.

How charming she was, how dignified, how tender to her merry little mother, this grave, handsome girl! He saw her, in fancy, opposite him at his table, moving so stately about his big empty house, filling it with pretty, useless woman's things, lighting every corner with that last touch of grace that the most faithful housekeeper could never hope to add to his lonely life. For Theodosia had taught him that he was lonely. He envied Dick this sister of his.

He wondered that marriage had never occurred to him before: simply it had not. Ever since that rainy day in April, twenty years ago, when they had buried the slender, soft-eyed little creature with his twisted silver ring on her cold finger, he had shut that door of life; and though it had been many years since the little ring had really bound him to a personality long faded from his mind, he had never thought to open the door—he had forgotten it was there.

He was not a talkative man, and, like many such, he dearly loved to be amused and entertained by others who were in any degree attractive to him. The picture of these two dear women adding their wit and charm and dainty way of living to his days grew suddenly very vivid to him; he realized that it was an unconscious counting on their continued interest and hospitality that had made the future so comfortable for so long.

With characteristic directness he began:

"Will your Ladyship allow me a half-hour of business with the queen-mother?"

She rose easily and stepped out through the long window to the little side porch, then to the lawn. They watched her as she paced slowly away from them, a tall violet figure vivid against all the green.

"She is a dear girl, isn't she?" said her mother softly.

A sudden flood of delighted pride surged through the colonel's heart. If only he might keep them happy and contented and — and his! He never thought of them apart: no rose and bud

on one stem were more essentially together than they.

"She is too dear for one to be satisfied
forever with even our charming neigh-
borliness," he answered gravely. "How
long have we lived 'across the street
from each other,' as they say here, Mrs.
Leroy?"

She did not raise her eyes from her
white ruffles.

"It is just a year this month," she
said.

"We are such good friends," he continued in his gentle, reserved voice,
"that I hesitate to break into such pleasant relations, even with the chance of
making us all happier, perhaps. But I
cannot resist the temptation. Could we
not make one family, we three?"

A quick, warm color flooded her
cheeks and forehead. She caught her
breath; her startled eyes met his with a
lightning-swift flash of something that
moved him strangely.

"What do you mean, Colonel Driscoll?" she asked, low and quickly.

"I mean, could you give me your daughter — if she — at any time — could think it possible?"

She drew a deep breath; the color seemed blown from her transparent skin like a flame from a lamp. For a moment her head seemed to droop; then she sat straight and moistened her lips, her eyes fixed level ahead.

"Lady?" she whispered, and he was sure that she thought the word was spoken in her ordinary tone. "Lady?"

"I know — I realize perfectly that it is a presumption in me — at my age — when I think of what she deserves. Oh, we won't speak of it again if you feel that it would be wrong!"

"No, no, it is not that," she murmured. "I — I have always known that I must lose her; but she — one is so selfish — she is all I have, you know!"

"But you would not lose her!" he

cried eagerly. "You would only share her with me, dear Mrs. Leroy! Do you think — could she — it is possible?"

"Lady is an unusual girl," she said evenly, but with something gone out of her warm, gay voice. "She has never cared for young people. I know that she admires you greatly. While I cannot deny that I should prefer less difference than lies between your ages, it would be folly in me to fail to recognize the desirability of the connection in every other way. Whatever her decision — and the matter rests entirely with her — my daughter and I are honored by your proposal, Colonel Driscoll."

She might have been reading a carefully prepared address: her eyes never wavered from the wall in front — it was as if she saw her words there.

"Then — then will you ask her?"

She stared at him now.

"You mean that you wish me to ask her to marry you?"

"Yes," he said simply. "She will feel freer in that way. You will know as I should not, directly, if there is any chance. I can talk about it with you more easily — somehow."

She shrugged her shoulders with a strange air of exhaustion; it was the yielding of one too tired to argue.

"Very well," she breathed, "go now, and I will ask her. Come this evening. You will excuse —"

She made a vague motion. The colonel pitied her tremendously in a blind way. Was it all this to lose a daughter? How she loved her!

"Perhaps to-morrow morning," he suggested, but she shook her head vehemently.

"No, to-night, to-night!" she cried. "Lady will know directly. Come to-night!"

He went out a little depressed. Already a tiny cloud hung between them. Suppose their pleasant waters had been troubled for worse than nothing? Suddenly his case appeared hopeless to him. What folly — a man of his years, and that fresh young creature with all her life before her! He wondered that he could have dreamed of it; he wished the evening over and the foolish mistake forgiven.

His sister was full of plans and dates, and her talk covered his almost absolute silence. After dinner she retired again into packing, and he strode through the dusk to the cottage; his had not been a training that seeks to delay the inevitable.

The two women sat, as usual at this hour, on the porch. Their white gowns shimmered against the dark honeysuckle-vine. He halted at the steps and took off the old fatigue-cap he sometimes wore, standing straight and tall before them.

Mrs. Leroy leaned back in her chair; the faintest possible gesture indicated her daughter, who had risen and stood beside her.

"Colonel Driscoll," she said in a low, uneven voice, "my daughter wishes me to say to you that she appreciates deeply the honor you do her, and that if you wish it she will be your wife. She — she is sure she will be happy."

The colonel felt his heart leap up and hit heavily against his chest. Was it possible? A great gratitude and pride glowed softly through him. He walked nearly up the steps and stood just below her, lifting her hand to his lips.

"My dear, dear child," he said slowly, "you give me too much, but you must not measure my thankfulness for the gift by my deserts. Whatever a man can do to make you and your mother happy shall be done so long as I live."

She smiled gravely into his eyes and bowed her head slightly; like all her little motions, it had the effect of a graceful ceremony. Then, slipping loose her hand, she seated herself on a low stool beside her mother's chair, leaning against her knee. Her sweet silence charmed him.

He took his accustomed seat, and they sat quietly, while the breeze puffed little gusts of honeysuckle across their faces. Occasional neighbors greeted them, strolling past; the newly watered lawns all along the street sent up a fresh turfy odor; now and then a bird chirped drowsily. He felt deliciously intimate, peacefully at home. A fine, subtle sense of *bien-être* penetrated his whole soul.

When he rose to go they had hardly exchanged a dozen words. As he held her hand closely, half doubting his right, she raised her face to him simply, and he kissed her white forehead. When he bent over her mother's hand it was as cold as stone.

Through the long pleasant weeks of the summer they talked and laughed and drove and sailed together, a happy trio. Mrs. Leroy's listless quiet of the first few days gave way to a brilliant, fitful gayety that enchanted the more silent two, and the few hours when she was not with them seemed incomplete. On his mentioning this to her one afternoon she shot him a strange glance.

"But this is all wrong," she said abruptly. "What will you do when I am gone in the winter?"

"What do you mean?" he asked. "Gone where, when, how?"

"My dear colonel," she said lightly, but with an obvious effort, "do you imagine that I cannot leave you a honeymoon, in spite of my doting parenthood? I plan to spend the latter part of the winter in New York with friends. Perhaps by spring —"

"My dear Mrs. Leroy, how absurd! How cruel of you! What will Lady do? What shall I do? She has never been separated from you in her life. Does she know of this?"

"No; I shall tell her soon. As for what she will do — she will have her husband. If that is not enough for her, she should not marry the man who cannot—"

She stopped suddenly and controlled with great effort a rising emotion almost too strong for her. Again a deep, inexplicable sympathy welled up in him. He longed to comfort her, to give her everything she wanted. He blamed himself and Jane for all the trouble they were causing her.

That afternoon she kept in her room, and he and his fiancée drank their tea together alone. He was worried by the news of the morning, dissatisfied out of all proportion, vexed that so sensible and natural a proposition should leave him so uneasy and disappointed. He had meant the smooth, quiet life to go on without a break, and now the new relation must change everything.

He glanced at Jane, a little irritated that she should not perceive his mood and exorcise it. But she had not her mother's marvellous susceptibility. She drank her tea in serene silence. He made a few haphazard remarks, hoping to lose in conversation the cloud that threatened his evening; but she only assented tranquilly and watched the changing colors of the early sunset.

"Have you made a vow to agree with everything I say?" he asked finally, half laughing, half in earnest.

"Not at all," she replied placidly, "but you surely do not want an argument?"

"Oh, no," he answered her, vexed at himself.

"What do you think of Mrs. ———'s novel?" he suggested, as the pages, fluttering in the rising breeze, caught his attention.

"Mother is reading it, not I," she returned indifferently. "I don't care very much for the new novels."

Involuntarily he turned as if to catch her mother's criticism of the book: light, perhaps, but witty, and with a little tang of harmless satire that always took his fancy. But she was not there. He sighed impatiently; was it possible he was a little bored?

A quick step sounded on the gravel walk, a swish of skirts.

"It is Louise Morris," she said, "I'll meet her at the gate."

After a short conference she returned.

"Will you excuse me, please?" she said, quite eagerly for her. "Mother will be down soon, anyway, I am sure. Louise's brother is back; he has been away in the West for six years. Mother will be delighted — she was always so fond of Jack. Louise is making a little surprise for him. He must be quite grown up now. I'll go and tell mother."

A moment later and she was gone. Mrs. Leroy took her place in the window, and imperceptibly under her gentle influence the cloud faded from his horizon; he forgot the doubt of an hour ago. At her suggestion he dined there, and found himself, as always when with his hostess, at his best. He felt that there was no hypocrisy in her interest in his ideas, and the ease with which he expressed them astonished him even while he delighted in it. Why could he not talk so with Jane? It occurred to him suddenly that it was because Jane herself talked rarely. She was, like him, a listener, for the most part. His mind, unusually alert and sensitive to-night, looked ahead to the happy winter evenings he had grown to count on so, and when, with an effort, he detached this third figure from the group to be so closely allied after Christmas-tide — the date fixed for the wedding — he perceived that there was a great gap in the picture, that the warmth and sparkle had suddenly gone. All the tenderness in the world could not disguise that flash of foresight.

He grew quiet, lost in revery. She, following his mood, spoke less and less;

and when Jane returned, late at night, escorted by a tall, bronzed young ranchman, she found them sitting in silence in a half-light, staring into the late September fire on the hearth.

In the month that followed an imperceptible change crept over the three. The older woman was much alone — variable as an April day, now merry and caressing, now sombre and withdrawn. The girl clung to her mother more closely, sat for long minutes holding her hand, threw strange glances at her betrothed that would have startled him, so different were they from her old, steady regard, had not his now troubled sense of some impalpable mist that wrapped them all grown stronger every day. He avoided sitting alone with her, wondering sometimes at the ease with which such tête-à-têtes were dispensed with. Then, struck with apprehension at his seeming neglect, he spent his ingenuity in delicate attentions toward her, courtly thoughtfulness of her tastes, beautiful gifts that provoked from her, in turn, all the little intimacies and tender friendliness of their earlier intercourse.

At one of these tiny crises of mutual restoration, she, sitting alone with him in the drawing-room, suddenly raised her eyes and looked steadily at him.

"You care for me, then, very much?" she said earnestly. "You — you would miss — if things were different? You really count on — on — our marriage? Are you happy?"

A great remorse rose in him. Poor child — poor, young, unknowing creature, that, after all, was only twenty-two! She felt it, then, the strange mist that seemed to muffle his words and actions, to hold him back. And she had given him so much!

He took her hands and drew her to him.

"My dear, dear child," he said gently, "forgive a selfish middle-aged bachelor if he cannot come up to the precious ideals of the sweetest girlhood in the world! I am no more worthy of you, Lady dear, than I have ever been, but I have never felt more tender toward you, more sensible of all you are giving me. I cannot pretend to the wild love of the poets you read so much; that time, if it ever was, is past for me. I am a plain, unromantic person, who takes and leaves a great deal for granted — I thought you knew that. But you must never doubt —" He paused a moment, and for the first time she interrupted him nervously.

"I never will — Clarence," she said almost solemnly; and it struck him for the first time that she had never called him by his name before. He leaned over her, and as in one of her rare concessions she lifted her face up to him, he bent lower than her forehead; what compelled him to kiss her soft cheek rather than her lips he did not know.

Unexpected business summoned him

to New York for a fortnight the next day, and the great city drew him irresistibly into its noisy maelstrom. The current of his thoughts changed absolutely. Old friends and new took up his leisure. His affairs, as they grew more pressing, woke in him a keen delight in the struggle with his opponents; as he shook hands triumphantly with his lawyer after a well-earned victory he felt years younger. He decided that he had moped too long in the country: "We must move into town this season," he said to himself.

He fairly ran up the cottage steps in the gathering dusk. He longed to see them, full of plans for the winter. Hannah met him at the door: the ladies had gone to a dance at the Morrises'; there had been an invitation for him, so he would not intrude if he followed.

Hastily changing his clothes, he walked up the street. Lights and music poured out of the open windows of the large house; the full moon made the grounds about it almost as bright as the rooms. He stepped up on the piazza and looked in at the swaying couples. Lady Jane, beautiful in pale blue mull, drifted by in her young host's arms. She was flushed with dancing; her hair had escaped from its usual calm. He hardly recognized her. As he looked out toward the old garden, he caught a glimpse of a flowing white gown, a lace scarf thrown over a head whose fine poise he could not mistake.

A young man passed him with a filmy crêpe shawl he knew well. The colonel stepped along with him.

"You are taking this to Mrs. Leroy?"

"Yes, colonel, she feels the air a little."

"Let me relieve you of it," and he walked alone into the garden with the softly scented cobweb over his arm.

She was standing in an old neglected summer-house, her back to the door. As he stopped behind her and laid the soft wrap over her firm white shoulders, she turned her head with a startled prescience of his personality, and met his eyes full. He looked straight into those soft gray depths, and as he looked, searching for something there, he knew not what, troubled strangely by her nearness and the helpless surrender of her fastened gaze, a great light burst upon him.

"It is you! it is you!" he said hoarsely, and crushing her in his arms, he kissed her heavily on her yielding mouth.

For a moment she rested against him. The music, piercingly sweet, drove away thought. Then she drew herself back, pushing him blindly from her.

"No, no, no!" she gasped, "it is Lady! You are mad —"

"Mad?" he said quickly. "I was never sane till now. When I think of what I had to offer that dear child, when I realize to what a farce of love I was sacrificing her — oh, Alice dearest, you are a woman; you must have known!"

She raised her head; an unquenchable triumph smiled at him.

"I did know!" she cried exultantly. Suddenly her whole expression changed, her head sank again.

"Oh, Lady, my child, my baby!" she moaned, all mother now, and broken-hearted.

"You must never tell her, never!" she panted. "You will forget; you—I will go away—"

"It is you who are mad, Alice," he said sternly. "Listen to me. For all these weeks it has been your voice I have remembered, your face I have seen in imagination in my house. It is you I have missed from us three—never Lady. It is you I have tried to please and hoped to satisfy—not Lady. Ever since you told me you would not spend the winter with us I have been discontented. Why, Alice, I have never kissed her in my life—as I have kissed you."

She grew red to the tips of her little

ears, and threw him a quick glance that tingled to his fingers' ends.

"You would not have me—oh, my dear, it is not possible!" he cried.

She burst into tears. "I don't know—I don't know!" she sobbed. "It will break her heart! I don't understand her any more; once I could tell what she would think, but not now."

"Hush! some one is coming," he warned her, and taking her arm he drew her out through a great gap in the side of the little house, so that they stood hidden by it.

"Then I will tell him to his face what I think of him!" said a young man's voice, angry, determined, but shaking with disappointment. "To hold a girl—"

"He does not hold me—I hold myself!" It was Lady's voice, low and trembling. "It is all my fault, Jack. I bound myself before I knew what—what a different thing it really was. I do love him — I love him dearly, but not — not — No, no; I don't mean what you think — or, if I do, I must not. Jack, I have promised, don't you see? And when I thought that perhaps he didn't care so much, and asked him — oh, I told you how beautifully he answered me. I will never hurt him so, never!"

"It is disgusting, it is horrible; he is twenty-five years older than you — he might be your father!" stormed the voice.

"I — I never cared for young people before!"

Could this be Lady, this shy, faltering girl? Moved by an overmastering impulse, the man behind the summer-house turned his head and looked through the broken wall.

Lady Jane was blushing and paling in quick succession: the waves of red flooded over her moved face and receded like the tide at turn. Her eyes were piteous; her hair fell low over her forehead; she looked incredibly young.

"Of course," said the young man bitterly, "it is a good match—a fine match. You will have a beautiful home and everything you want."

She put out her hands appealingly. "Oh, Jack, how can you hurt me so? You know I would live with you in a garret—on the plains—"

"Then do it."

"I shall never hurt a person so terribly to whom I have freely given my word," she said, with a touch of her old-time decision.

Colonel Driscoll felt his blood sweeping through his veins like wine. He was far too excited for finesse, too eager—and he had been so willing to wait, once!—for the next sweet moment when this almost tragedy should be resolved into its elements. He strode out into the open space in front of the little house.

"My dear young people," he said, as they stared at him in absolute silence, "I am, I am—" He had intended to carry

[213]

the matter off jocularly, but the sight of the girl's tear-stained face and the emotion of the minutes before had softened and awed him. His eyes seemed yet to hold those gray ones; he felt strangely the pressure of that soft body against his.

"Ah, my dear," he said gently, "could you not believe me when I told you that my one wish was to make you happy as long as I lived? Happiness is not built on mistakes, and you must forgive us if we do not always allow youth to monopolize them.

"She has always been like a dear child to me, Mr. Morris"—he turned to the other man—"and you would never wish me to change my regard for her, could you know it!

"Go with him, Lady dear, and forgive me if I have ever pained you—believe me, I am very happy to-night."

He raised her softly as she knelt before him weeping, and kissed her hair.

“ But there is nothing to forgive,” he assured her.

They went away hand in hand, happy, like two dazed children for whom the sky has suddenly but not—because they are young—too miraculously opened, and the shrubbery swallowed them.

He turned and strode back into the shadow. Mrs. Leroy sat crouching on the fallen timber, her head still bent. Stooping behind her, he drew her toward him.

“ They have forgotten us by now,” he whispered, “ can I make you forget them ? ”

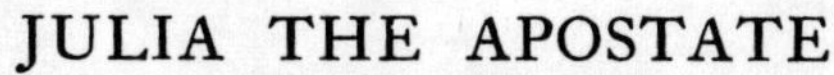

JULIA THE APOSTATE

JULIA THE APOSTATE

"YOU don't think it's too young for me, girls?"

"Young for you — *par exemple!* I should say not," her niece replied, perking the quivering aigrette still more obliquely upon her aunt's head. Carolyn used *par exemple* as a good cook uses onion — a hint of it in everything. There were those who said that she interpolated it in the Litany; but Carolyn, who was born Caroline and a Baptist, was too much impressed by the liturgy of what she called The Church to insert even an uncanonized comma.

"Now don't touch it, Aunt Julia, for it's deliciously chic, and if you had your way you'd flatten it down right straight in the middle — you know you would."

Miss Trueman pursed her lips quizzically.

" I've always thought, Carrie — *lyn*," she added hastily, as her niece scowled, " that they put things askew to make 'em different — for a change, as you might say. Now, if they're *never* in the middle, it's about as tiresome, isn't it?"

Elise, whose napkin-ring bore malignant witness to her loving aunt, Eliza Judd, laughed irrepressibly : she had more sense of humor than her sister. It was she who, though she had assisted in polishing the old copper kettle subsequently utilized as a holder for the tongs and shovel, had refused to consider the yet older wash-boiler in the light of a possible coal-scuttle, greatly to the relief of her aunt, who blushed persistently at any mention of the hearth.

She patted the older woman encouragingly.

"That's right, Aunt Ju-ju, argue it out!" she advised.

Miss Trueman winced. She had never accustomed herself to those senseless monosyllables that parodied her name; nor could she understand the frame of mind that found them preferable to the comfortable "Aunt Jule" of the old days.

"Ju-ju!" Strips of unwholesome flesh-colored paste, sugar-sprinkled, dear to her childish heart but loathed by a maturer palate, rose to her mind. There had been another haunting recollection: for months she had been unable to define it perfectly, though it had always brought a thrill of disgust with its vague appeal. One day she caught it and told them.

"It was that dreadful creature Mr. Barnum exhibited," she declared, "that we didn't allow the children to go to see —Jo-jo, the Dog-faced Boy! You remember?"

Their cold horror, briefly expressed, had shown her that she had trespassed too far on their indulgence, and she spoke of it no more, but the memory rankled.

"It's so strange you don't see how cunning it is," Carolyn complained; "everybody does it now. The whole Chatworth family have those names, Aunt Ju, and it is the dearest thing to hear the old doctor call Captain Arthur 'Ga-ga.' You know that dignified sister with the lovely silvery hair? Well, they all call her 'Looty.' And nobody thinks of Hunter Chatworth's real name —he's always 'Toto.'"

"And he has three children!"

Miss Trueman sighed; the constitution of the modern family amazed her endlessly. Ga-ga, indeed!

"Do the children call him Toto, too?" she demanded, with an attempt at sarcasm, a conversational form to which she was by nature a stranger.

"Oh, I don't know about that," Carolyn answered carelessly. "I suppose not. Though plenty of children do, you know. Mrs. Ranger's little girl always calls her mother Lou."

"Mrs. Ranger — you mean the woman that smokes?"

Miss Trueman's tone brought vividly to the mind a person dangling from disgusted finger-tips a mouse or beetle.

"For heaven's sake, Aunt Jule" — in moments of intense exasperation they reverted unconsciously to the old form — "don't speak of her as if she smoked for a living!"

"I should rather not speak of her at all," said Miss Trueman severely.

They raised their eyebrows helplessly: Carolyn's irritation was so unfeigned that she omitted a justly famous shrug.

For two years they had devoted an appreciable part of their busy hours to modifying Aunt Julia's antique prejudices, developing in her the latent æsthetic sense that their Wednesday art class taught them existed in every one, cajoling her into a tolerance of certain phases of modern literature considered seriously and weekly by the Monday Afternoon Club, and incidentally utilizing her as a chaperon and housekeeper in their modest up-town apartment.

The first six months of her sojourn had been almost entirely occupied with accustoming herself to the absence of an attic and a cellar; long days of depression they learned, finally, to trace to this incredible source. Later she dealt with the problem of subsisting from eight till one on two rolls and a cup of coffee; successfully, in the ultimate issue, as surreptitious bits of fried ham and buckwheat cakes, with suspicious odors, winked at discreetly by her nieces, witnessed. It would have been unkind, as Elise suggested, to criticise Aunt Ju-ju's performances at the ungodly hour of seven in the morning, when their own correctly Continental repast, flanked by a chrysanthemum in a tall vase, not only tallied so accurately with their digestive and æsthetic necessities, but appeared, moreover, with such gratifying regularity one hour later.

Both Carolyn and her sister had inherited from their mother, Miss Trueman's older sister, a real gift for teaching, and this, rather than their respective abilities in art and music, enabled them to impart very successfully the elements of these necessary branches to the young ladies of a fashionable boarding-school just outside the city.

It was politely regretted by their friends that they were unable to give themselves unreservedly to the exercise of their art without the cramping necessity for teaching; but it is probable that both the girls estimated their not too extraordinary talents very sensibly, though far from displeased by a more flattering judgment.

Miss Trueman, who possessed the characteristic veneration of the bred and born New Englander for his native or imported school-ma'am, resented persistently their somewhat patronizing attitude toward the profession second only to the ministry in her stanch respect. A little of the simple grandeur of those childhood days when "the teacher boarded with them" clung with the ineradicable force of habit to her mind, and she could not understand their restive attitude at "the fine positions as teachers Hattie's girls have got."

"I'm sure you make more money than that Miss Seymour that gets her own meals in her room—she said so herself."

"Oh, well, there are other things to be considered, Aunt Ju; and, anyway, she's a real bohemian, Polly Seymour. There's a fascination in it."

"There's no fascination in being hungry that I can see, and she admitted that, L—Elise," Miss Trueman insisted severely. "I don't understand how she could have done it — I would have died first. And she seemed to think it was a great joke to have her friends give her a dinner — I think it was terrible."

"Why, Aunt Jule, how ridiculous! We were delighted to do it — it was perfectly dear of her to let us, too. And think of the people we met there — Rawlins and Mr. Ware! You don't mind being poor if such men will come just out of interest in you, I tell you. Do you remember, Elise, how Mr. Rawlins called her 'little girl'? Mr. Ware lets her use his models whenever she likes, too," Carolyn added respectfully.

"Oh, she's bound to arrive!" Elise agreed.

Aunt Ju-ju sniffed uncontrolledly.

"I should hope she'd arrive at the point where she could buy her own dinners," she remarked. "To be beholden for your bread" . . .

Here were two points of view as little

likely to coincide as the parallel lines of science, and at some such stage as this the discussions were wont to cease.

To-day the apartment was swept and garnished for a social function long planned by the nieces. Carnations leaned from tall glass vases, intricate little cakes jostled carefully piled sandwiches, and a huge brass samovar, borrowed for the occasion, gave dignity to the small parlor. Miss Trueman had learned by now the unwritten law that prevented the various objects in the once proudly segregated " drawing-room set " from association with each other, and made no attempt to correct their intentional isolation. The samovar she refused utterly to meddle with, assuring them that she would as soon think of running a locomotive.

As the guests began to arrive Miss Trueman found herself regarding them even more critically than usual; an argumentative spirit rose in her, and her calm contradiction of Mrs. Ranger, who discussed with great subtlety the notable advantages—even from the artistic point of view—of the approaching spring when experienced in the city, in comparison with that be-rhymed season's vaunted country beauties, startled more than one person.

"Just because they're more delicate, just because you must look harder to discover them, just because you must get as much from a pot of hyacinths on the Avenue as from a whole field of primroses in the backwoods, you know," she concluded, and the little circle nodded sagely and congratulated themselves on an unpublished paragraph.

"I don't agree with you, Mrs. Ranger," said Aunt Ju-ju flatly, to the absolute amazement of her nieces and the tolerant amusement of the assembly. "I guess you haven't lived in the country much, or you wouldn't talk so. And primroses don't grow in fields here, anyway. If you could see my hyacinths and crocuses

in round beds at home, you wouldn't
mention those poor little stalks in the
pots."

Mrs. Ranger laughed, and directed her
searching, level glance at the older woman, who combined in her comely, un-
disguised middle age something at once
more matronly and more childish than
the analytic authoress could ever find in
her own mirror.

"Aha!" she cried, "then you are no
friend of dear old Horace, after all, Miss
Trueman! He and I, you see—"

The relation of these two urbanites
was revealed no further, for a bustle in
the little hall drew attention to a new-
comer unknown not only to the guests
but evidently to the hostesses, who rose,
smiling uncertainly, as a portly, broad-
shouldered man with iron-gray hair made
his way through the group about the
samovar.

"I'll have to introduce myself, I see,"
he began, not precisely with what an exi-

gent society calls ease of manner, but with a certain practical self-possession quite as effective.

"I didn't expect the girls to remember me, but I thought perhaps you might, Julia."

Miss Trueman peered out from the shaded five-o'clock gloom so dear to Carolyn's soul.

"I don't seem—it's not—why, Cousin Lorando Bean, it's not you?"

"That's it," he said heartily, "that's just exactly it. And he's mighty glad to see some of his relations again, I can tell you. And these are Carrie and Lizzie, I suppose. Well, well, fifteen years is a long time, even to an old fellow like me, and you girls were just beginning to be young ladies when I left Connecticut. How are you all?"

If this simple greeting came like a breath of her native air to Miss Trueman, it cannot be said to have had a similar effect on her nieces. Courtesy

prevented a full expression of their feel-
ings, but they affected no undue delight
at the presence of their new-found relative — whom they had very sincerely forgotten, along with many other details of
a somewhat inartistic youth — and turned
to their other guests with a frank relief
when they had established him, with a
cup of tea, a sandwich, and Aunt Julia,
in the near-by dining-room.

"A third or fourth cousin, I believe,
who has lived a long time in the West,"
they explained. The company, some
of whom doubtless possessed third or
fourth cousins from the West, nodded
comprehensively, and the interrupted
function flowed smoothly on again.

Cousin Lorando Bean balanced his
cup on his broad palm and gazed about
appreciatively at the casts and water-colors
on the dull green walls.

"Very snug little quarters, these," he
volunteered, "but, do you know, Cousin
Jule, I suppose it's all right for ladies,

but I don't seem to breathe extra well in these little rooms, somehow! I've been in two or three of them like this, more or less, since I came to New York — people I used to know that I've been hunting up — and, by George, I began to feel as if I was getting red in the face, if you see what I mean."

"Yes, indeed, Cousin Lorando, I do," returned Miss Trueman eagerly, "I see exactly. And not having any cellar — you've no idea! Nor any attic, either. And often and often we have the gas lighted all through breakfast. Of course there are a great many conveniences," she added loyally, "and there's no doubt it saves steps. But I almost think I'd rather take 'em."

He nodded.

"What's become of the old place, Cousin Jule? I judge you've been out of it some time?"

"Two years, Cousin Lorando. The girls had been boarding up to then, and when Aunt Martha died they got up this plan for me to come down and live with them, for they couldn't afford it quite, alone, and then I could chaperon them."

Aunt Julia delivered herself of this phrase with a certain complacency. Mr. Bean looked up sharply.

"That means that nobody gets a show to abduct 'em while you're around, I take it?" he inquired.

"We-ell, not exactly," she demurred.

"But that's the idea? I thought so. Yes. How old is Lizzie now? Thirty?"

"Oh, no, Cousin Lorando; L—Elise isn't twenty-nine yet. Carolyn is about thirty."

"I don't seem to recall any one chaperoning you and Hattie when you were thirty," he suggested thoughtfully.

She laughed involuntarily.

"Oh, Hattie was married, Cousin Lorando, and the children were ten years old! And, anyway, it was different then."

"The girls were just as pretty, I guess," he insisted. "And there were plenty of buggies, if anybody had designs."

There was a pause, and the buzz of voices from the other room rose loudly.

"They've neither of them got their mother's looks," he observed; and then, with apparent irrelevance: "When will they be considered safe to go about alone?"

"I don't know exactly what you mean," she began a little coldly, but his laugh reassured her.

"Oh, yes, you do," he contradicted, "and don't you be getting cross at your Cousin Lorando Bean! You know I always loved to tease you; it made your eyes snap — and it does now."

"How can you?" She looked reproachfully at him.

"And I tell you this, Cousin Jule: neither of those girls will ever get up a color like that!"

She shook her head, but she was not displeased. He took out a fat chocolate-colored cigar and fingered it wistfully.

"I suppose I mustn't smoke?" he queried.

Her quick answer surprised herself.

"I should hope you could, if that woman can!"

"Which one?"

"That Mrs. Ranger, the one near the samovar — that big brass thing. Liz — Elise didn't introduce her to you. They don't introduce people the way they do at home, Cousin Lorando — I hope you didn't mind. They think it's awkward."

"Oh, Lord, no, I don't mind. I can spare her, anyway. She's checked up too high for me. But she can look you through pretty thoroughly, can't she?"

"She writes books," Miss Trueman returned, the finality of her tone indicating that she had explained any possible idiosyncrasy of the lady in question.

"Oh, I see. And the little red-haired one, does she write books, too?"

"No; she's an artist. She smokes too, though. Not cigars, like yours, but cigarettes. She's supposed to be a very good painter, but she doesn't make what Carrie—lyn makes. The girls have very good positions in Miss Abrams' school."

"Um, what do they get, now?"

Miss Trueman mentioned the modest sum with pride.

"And then with my money and what we get from the rent of the place — the girls and I each have a third, you know — we do very nicely."

"So you rented the place?"

"Yes, Cousin Lorando, though I hated to. But I wouldn't sell it, though they wanted me to. I just couldn't."

"I know."

He lighted his cigar and puffed at it in meditative silence for a moment, while the babble from the parlor floated in with the odor of the Ceylon tea and cigarettes.

"That's what I came about, Cousin Jule — the old place. You may think it's queer, for I never lived there but two years once, when father and your Uncle Joe farmed it on shares; but those two years just made it home to me. Of course Uncle Joe wasn't any real relation of mine, and you-all weren't my real cousins, but it was the only family I ever had, so to say, and I loved every one of you. Then we moved back into town; but you know I came in every week or so, and Aunt Martha used to have my room in the attic ready for me, just the same."

"Yes, I know; Aunt Martha never forgot you, Cousin Lorando."

"Well, it's fifteen years since I saw the old place, and a lot's happened since then, I tell you. First place, I'm a rich man, Cousin Jule.

"Oh, I don't mean one of these multimillionaires you have about here, for I haven't even seven figures opposite my name; but short of that I did very well for myself out West there, and I earned it all fair, too — though I was pretty lucky, and that counts.

"Anyhow, never mind about that. Only I've got enough to have anything I want, and to give my friends something, too. So as soon as I got back East I went straight down to the farm. But it was all shut up and a kind of green hedge where the fence used to be, and I judged it was sold, and I felt pretty sore about it, so I came right away."

"They only come there in June," Miss Trueman explained, "and they go back before Thanksgiving."

"Yes. Well, I didn't know that."

He waited again for a few seconds, and Miss Trueman sat in respectful silence till he should continue.

"You see, I'd been East once before,

eight years ago, but I didn't see the farm then," he said finally.

"I got married while I was West."

His audience of one started slightly.

"She's dead now," he added abruptly.

"Oh, Cousin Lorando —"

"You needn't bother about the sympathy, my dear, for there's none needed. I hadn't been with her for a good while. I saw her in a concert-hall out there, and she had curly hair and a kind of taking way with her, and so I married her. I'd just made a big hit, and she wanted to come to New York, and we came. We went to a big hotel, and it was dress-suits for me and diamonds for her, and we drove in a carriage in the park in the afternoon. She liked it, but I soon got enough. I don't care much for that sort of thing. She wanted to go to the theatre and see the girls that she'd been one of, you see, from the other side of the curtain. And she saw a man there she used to know, and — well, it turned out she liked him better, that's all."

"Oh, Cousin Lorando, how terrible — for her!"

"Um, yes. She didn't think it was specially terrible, I guess, though. She just packed up and went."

"Went?"

"Yes — with him, you see. Diamonds and all. I got a divorce, of course. And she wasn't such a bad lot, after all, for he hadn't any money to speak of, compared to me. It was the man she wanted. Well, she got him."

"How awful!" Miss Trueman murmured.

"Oh, yes, I felt pretty sick for a while. But we hadn't been any too happy before she saw him, you see. It was a big mistake. She wasn't exactly the kind of woman you'd be apt to know, you see. So perhaps I got off easier than I deserved. But I never would have married while she was alive. Not but what I had a right to, you understand, but I guess I'm old-fashioned more ways than one. I read about her death a year or so ago. I don't believe she had any too good a time herself. She had an awful temper. But she certainly did have pretty hair," he concluded thoughtfully.

Miss Trueman gasped.

"So I didn't want to see New York again; I just hated the place. And this time I only came because I found out you and the girls were here, and you were about all there was left. People die so. And I wanted to find out about the old place. I wanted to buy it, if I could, when I thought it was sold."

"But, Cousin Lorando, I couldn't sell it!"

"Oh, no, I s'pose not. Still, I might buy out the girls' thirds and rent yours, couldn't I? I'd pay you as much and more than anybody else would, I guess. And you could keep your interest. And keep half of the house, for that matter, to use when you wanted — it's big enough."

"Why, yes, I don't see why I couldn't

do that," she said thoughtfully. "That would be nice."

"You see, I'm willing to make any arrangement, Cousin Jule. It's about all there is that I'm fond of now, that old place. I haven't any folks of my own, and not a chick nor child, and I love every stick and stone of that farm. I love the country, and I love Connecticut country best of all, I don't care if it is rocky. You can't make farming pay in New England any more. But I don't need to make it pay; I'm willing to pay for the pleasure of it. And I want to do something for the town, too. I want 'em to be glad I came to settle there. Who's got the keys?"

"I have, right here," she answered. "The furniture is all ours, you see; they haven't brought much, only they've changed things all around. I haven't renewed the lease yet for this year."

"Well, now, look here, Jule," Mr. Bean cried eagerly, dropping the end of his cigar into a bonbon-dish on the little side-table, "why don't you run right up there with me to-night, and we'll look it all over and sort of plan it out? We can go up on the six-thirty, and get there by half-past ten, and stop at the hotel, and be there all ready to look it over to-morrow. Now, how's that?"

"Why, but, Cousin Lorando—I— there isn't time—I hadn't planned—"

"Lord, neither had I, but what's the difference? If you want a thing done, go and do it yourself. Wouldn't you like to go? It's lovely up there; the spring's coming on fast, you know. I got lots of pussy-willow, and some little fellows told me there were May-flowers somewhere. You'll see more grass in a minute there than you can hunt up here in a week. Come on, Cousin Jule!"

"I believe I will!" said Miss Trueman, with conviction.

"Just pack up a bag for your aunt, Carrie, while I get a cab," said Mr.

Bean from the doorway. " We're going up to the old place—I'm thinking of buying it. I expect we'll be back to-morrow."

" Your cousin appears to be a person of decision," Mrs. Ranger suggested to the still dazed Elise, as the cab rolled away.

" I don't understand Aunt Ju-ju at all," Carolyn interpolated crossly. She had not been in the habit of packing her aunt's bag. " She usually makes such a fuss about starting to go anywhere—days ahead, in fact. And now at fifteen minutes' notice! And her best gown!"

" It makes a difference, having a man to run it," said the novelist sagely.

When two days had passed and their aunt had not yet appeared, her nieces were not unnecessarily alarmed, for her attachment to her old home was great, and it required no unusual degree of imagination to picture her delighted lingering over the old things, her purposely prolonged transaction of business details. But four days of unexplained absence had its effect upon their own little ménage; and when a week's visit had been accomplished and their beseeching letters had elicited only vague postal cards explaining nothing, but suggesting their presence at the farm, they became convinced of the necessity for action on their part, and went, more or less in the presumable spirit of the mountain in search of the fractious Prophet.

Tired and cross after four hours' travel on an incredibly hot 1st of April, they walked sternly up the board walk that led to the old-style porch, to be greeted by their cousin, who sat in snowy shirt-sleeves, tilted back in his chair against the house, smoking his fat, dark cigar.

"Welcome home, girls — glad to see you!" he called cheerily. "Here they are, Jule! Now don't be afraid, but come right out and see them!"

"Why, bless your heart, Lorando, I'm not afraid," a familiar voice answered; and Aunt Julia appeared before them, cool in blue checked gingham, with an enveloping white apron and familiarly floury hands.

"I'm just beating up some biscuit for tea," she explained, "but I guess you can shake hands with me, girls"; and as she extended both arms hospitably they saw upon her floured left hand an unmistakable shining gold band.

"Aunt Jule!" they gasped together. "Are you—is it—"

"That's it exactly," said Cousin Lorando Bean. "She is. And I hope you'll congratulate her, girls, though nobody knows better than I what a good housekeeper you've lost! I'll tell you the facts of the matter, and you can judge for yourself. If ever two people were made for each other, those two are your Aunt Jule and me. We love the country, and we love this farm, and what's very important, we love the same way of living."

"That's quite true, Carrie—lyn," Aunt Julia interposed, the tears in her eyes, but a new decision in her voice.

"I like my tea at night, and so does your Cousin Lorando. And I should have wanted gravy on my potato if I lived to be a hundred. And, Carrie, I *could not live* without a cellar!

"And if you knew how nervous I got when that old dumb-waiter in the kitchen used to whistle for the things to be put on it! I used to hate it so—sometimes I'd wake up in the night and think I heard it! Once I lost my temper at it, and I answered it back: 'I haven't anything to go down, and I wouldn't give it to you if I had!'"

"Why, Aunt Jule!" they cried.

"And I tell you, Carrie, when you have cleaned house regularly, spring and fall, for forty years, ever since you were born, it makes an awful break to give it up! And I do love a good crayon portrait."

They looked at each other in silence.

"And when you have a set of furniture, it makes me nervous not to have it set together," Aunt Julia went on determinedly.

"And I will *not* have a woman smoking in my house!

"And oh, Carrie, if you knew how I suffered with that dirty darky girl!"

"But — but, Aunt Jule, why didn't you —"

"You see, Carrie and Lizzie, it was this way," said Mr. Bean soothingly.

"Your aunt and I got talking old times, and we found that we both felt about the same. And after we'd looked the old house over together a day or two, she couldn't seem to leave it, somehow, and she couldn't live in it alone, and I always wanted it.

"So I said, 'If you'll just step over to the parson's, across the street, with me, we'll fix this all right in about ten minutes. You've known me ever since I was a boy, and I've known you, and it's nobody's business but ours if we want to finish up together.' I may have said a few other things, too, but that's neither here nor there. And when she said what would the girls do, I told her that what with the full price of their interest in the farm, and her third that she could add to it — for a sort of wedding-present, you see — I didn't see but what you could well afford to take a trip to Europe and stay about as long as you liked — she said you wanted to do that more than anything; though why I don't know — Connecticut ought to be good enough for anybody!"

They sank upon the porch steps, sincerely overcome.

" I knew you'd like it when you came to know it all," said Aunt Julia placidly. " He's the kindest man —"

And to their excited eyes the very

tidies on the geometrically arranged chairs, the bright rag rugs on the floor, the biscuits and preserves consecrated to their New England tea, yes, even the insistent shirt-sleeves of Cousin Lorando Bean, were lighted by a halo of content.

MRS. DUD'S SISTER

MRS. DUD'S SISTER

THEY were having tea on the terrace. As Varian strolled up to the group he wished that Hunter could see the picture they made — Hunter, who had not been in America for thirty years, and who had been so honestly surprised when Varian had spoken of Mrs. Dud's pretty maids — she always had pretty ones, even to the cook's third assistant.

"Maids? Maids? It used to be 'help,'" he had protested. "You don't mean to say they have waitresses in Binghamville now?"

Varian had despaired of giving him any idea.

"Come over and see Mrs. Dud," he

had urged, "and do her portrait. We've moved on since you left us, you know. She's a wonder — she really is. When you remember how she used to carry her father's dinner to the store Saturday afternoons —"

"And now I suppose she sports real Mechlin on her cap," assented Hunter, anxious to show how perfectly he caught the situation.

Varian had roared helplessly. "Cap? Cap!" he had moaned finally. "Oh, my sainted granny! Cap! My poor fellow, your view of Binghamville must be like the old maps of Africa in the green geography, that said 'desert' and 'interior' and 'savage tribes' from time to time. I should like awfully to see Mrs. Dud in a cap."

Hunter had looked puzzled.

"But, dear me! she might very well wear one, I should think," he had murmured defensively. "I don't wish to be invidious, but surely Lizzie must be —

let's see ; 'eighty, 'ninety — why, she must be between forty-five and fifty now."

Varian had waved his hand dramatically. " Nobody considers Mrs. Dud and time in the same breath. If you could see her in her golf rig ! Or on a horse ! She even sheds a lustre on the rest of us. I forget my rheumatism ! "

But Hunter, retreating behind his determination to avoid a second seasickness — it might have been sincere; nobody ever knew — had stayed in Florence, and Varian had been obliged to come without him to the house-party.

On a straw cushion, a cup in her strong white hand, a bunch of adoring young girls at her feet, sat Mrs. Dud. Rosy and firm-cheeked, crisp in stiff white duck, deliciously contrasted with her fluffy Parisian parasol, she scorned the softening ruffles of her presumable contemporaries ; her delicately squared chin, for the most part held high, showed a straight white collar under a throat only a little fuller than the girlish ones all around her.

Old Dudley himself strolled about the group, gossiping here and there with some pretty woman, sending the grave servants from one to another with some particularly desirable sandwich, "rubbing it in," as he said to the men who had failed to touch his score on the links, tantalizingly uncertain as to which one of the young women he would invite to lead the cotillon with him at the club dance that week : none of the young men could take his place at that, as themselves enviously admitted.

What a well-matched couple it was ! What a lot they got out of life ! Varian walked quietly by the group, to enjoy better the pretty, modish picture they made. Their quick chatter, their bursts of laughter, the sweet faint odor of the tea, the gay dresses and light flannels, with the quiet, sombrely attired servants to add tone, all gave him, fresh from

Hunter's quick sense of the effective, an appreciation that gained force from his separateness ; he walked farther away to get a different point of view.

He was out of any path now, and suddenly, hardly beyond reach of their voices, he found himself in a part of the grounds he had never approached before. A thick high hedge shut in a kind of court at the side and back of the great house, and a solid wooden door, carefully matched to its green, left open by accident, showed a picture so out of line with the succession of vivid scenes that dazzled the visitor at Wilton Bluffs that he stopped involuntarily. The rectangle was carpeted with the characteristic emerald turf of the place, divided by intersecting red brick paths into four regular squares. In the farther corner of each of these a trim green clothes-tree was planted, all abloom with snowy fringed napkins that shone dazzling white against the hedge. One of the squares was a

neat little kitchen-garden; parsley was
there in plenty, and other vaguely familiar green things, curly-leaved and spear-
pointed. A warm gust of wind brought
mint to his nostrils. A second plot held
a small crab-apple tree covered with pink
and orange globes. A great tortoise-shell
cat with two kittens ornamented the
third, and in the middle of the fourth, beside a small wooden table, a woman sat
with her back toward the intruder. On
the table were one or two tin boxes and
a yellow earthen dish; in her left hand,
raised to the shoulder-level, was a tall
thin bottle, from which an amber fluid
dripped in an almost imperceptibly thin
stream; her right arm stirred vigorously.
She was a middle-aged woman with
lightly grayed hair—a kind of premoni-
tory powdering. Over her full skirt of
lavender-striped cotton stuff fell a broad,
competent white apron. Except for the
thudding of the spoon against the bowl,
and a faint, homely echo of clashing

china and tin, mingled with occasionally raised voices and laughter from some farther kitchen region, all was utterly, placidly still.

Varian stood chained to the open gate. Something in the calm sun-bathed picture tugged strongly at his heart. He thought suddenly of his mother and his Aunt Delia—he had been very fond of Aunt Delia. And what cookies she used to make! Molasses cookies, brown, moist, and crumbly, they had sweetened his boyhood.

What was it, that delighted sense of congruity that filled him, every passing second, with keener familiarity, so strangely tinged with sorrow and regret? Ah, he had it! He bit his lip as it came clear to him. His little namesake nephew, dead at eight years old, and dear as only a dearly loved child can be, had delighted greatly in the Kate Greenaway pictures that came in " painting-books," with colored prints on alternate pages and corresponding outlines on the others. Dozens of those books the boy had cleverly filled in with his little japanned paint-box and mussy, quill-handled brushes; and the scene before him, the rich tints of the hedge, the symmetrical little tree brilliant with hundreds of tiny globes, the big white apron, the lazy yellow cats, and everywhere the prim rectangular lines so amusingly conventional to accentuate the likeness, almost choked him with the suddenness of the recognition. They must have colored that very picture a dozen times, Tommy and he.

Half unconsciously he rested his arms on the top of the gate and drifted into revery. He forgot that he was at Wilton Bluffs, one of the greatest of the country palaces, and lived for a while in a mingled vision of his boyhood on the old farm and in the land of the Greenaway painting-books.

Suddenly a door opened into the green.

A housemaid advanced to the table, bearing in both red hands a long tray covered with a napkin. On the napkin lay, heaped in rich confusion, a great pile of spicy, smoking brown cookies.

"They're just out o' the oven," she began, but Varian could contain himself no longer. He could not be deceived: he would have known those cookies in the Desert of Sahara. He crossed the little plot in three long steps, and faced the astonished maid.

"I beg your pardon," he said firmly, "but it is very necessary that I should have one of those cookies! I hope you can spare one?"

She giggled convulsively.

"I—I guess you can, sir," she murmured, laying down the tray and retreating toward the house door.

Varian faced the older woman, and, with hat still in hand, instinctively bowed lower; for this was no housekeeper— he was sure of that. Even as she met his eyes a great flood of pink rushed to her smooth forehead, and she dropped her lids as she bowed slightly. He reflected irrelevantly that he had never seen Mrs. Dudley blush in his life.

"You are very welcome to all you wish, I am sure," she said graciously. "I — I didn't know any one liked them but me. I always have them made for me — I taught her the rule. I always call them" — she laughed nervously, and it dawned on him that this woman was really shy and "talking against time," as they said — "I always call them 'Aunt Delia's cookies.' They — "

"Aunt Delia's cookies!" he interrupted. "What Aunt Delia?"

"Aunt Delia Parmentre," she returned, a little surprised, evidently, at this stranger, who, with a straw sailor-hat in one hand and a warm molasses cooky in the other, stared so intently at her. "She wasn't really my aunt, of course — "

"But she was mine!" he burst out,

"and these are her cookies, and no mistake.   Who are you?"

Again she flushed, but more lightly.

"I am Miss Redding," she said with a gentle dignity, "Mrs. Wilton's sister."

He stared at her vaguely.

"Mrs. Wilton—oh! you're her sister?   I didn't know—"   He stopped abruptly.   As his confusion grew, her own faded away.

"You didn't know she had one?" she asked, almost mischievously.

"I didn't know you were here," he recovered himself.   "You've never been with Mrs. Dud before, have you?"

"No, not here when there was company," she said.

He hardly noticed the words; his mind was groping among past histories.

"Her sister—her sister," he muttered.   "Why, then," with an illuminating smile, "I used to go to school with you!   I'm Tom Varian!"

She smiled and held out her hand.

"I'm very glad to see you," she said cordially. "Won't you—" She looked about for a chair, but he dropped on the grass at her feet.

"You've changed since we met last," he remarked, biting into his cooky. She looked at his bronzed face and thick silvered hair and nodded thoughtfully.

"I was six years old then," she said; "and you were one of the 'big boys'— you were fourteen."

"That's a long while," he suggested laughingly.

"It is thirty-six years," she replied simply.

He winced. His associates were not accustomed to be so scrupulously accurate. It seemed indecently long ago. And yet there was a certain charm, now one faced it, a quaint halo of interest.

"You used to hand me water in a tin dipper," he said.

She nodded. "Yes, that was for a reward, when I was good," she said seriously. "I could hand the water to the big boys. I was very proud of it. You drank a great deal."

He chuckled. "I was born thirsty," he acknowledged. "By George, how it comes back! I can see it now, that school-house! Funny little red thing— remember how it looked? Big shelf around the sides for a desk, and another under that for the books? Bench all round the room to sit on, and we just whopped our legs over and faced round to recite? And carved— Lord! I don't believe there was an inch of the wood, all told, that was clear! I nearly cut my thumb off there, one day."

"One of the big girls fainted away," she added, "and they laid her on the floor and told me to bring a dipper of water; but my hand shook so I spilled it all over my apron, and she came to before we got more. I was very timid."

He began on another cooky.

"Did you have two pigtails? And

striped stockings?" he inquired, his eyes fixed reminiscently on the hedge.

She nodded softly.

"And played some game with stones? I can't just remember—"

"It was houses," she reminded him. "We little girls used to make little houses—just marked out with stones in squares on the ground; and if you boys felt like it, you'd bring us big flat stones to eat our dinner on."

"Ah, yes!" It all came back to him. "And then you'd race off to get flag-root or something, and—"

"And gobble our dinner as we ran. It was fun, all the same," she added.

"But what a mite you were, to be in school!" he said wonderingly. "What under heaven did you study?"

"I don't remember at all," she confessed. "But I suppose I spelled. Do you remember the spelling-matches? And how you big ones wanted to 'leave off head'?"

He chuckled. "I should say I did! And sometimes the greatest idiot would 'leave off head' because there wasn't any more time. It was maddening!"

He munched in silence for a while, and she did not dream of interrupting.

"In the winter, though—George! but it was cold! We used to positively swim through the drifts. I tell you, there aren't any such snows now! How did you get there?"

"I only went in the summer," she said; "and I used to come in all stained with the berries I ate along the way. It was dreadful"—she grew stern, as if addressing the little girl in striped stockings and pigtails—"the way I ate berries! I used to eat the bushes clean on the way to school!"

She had got over her first shyness, and had gained time to realize her big apron, which she hastily untied. He caught the motion and protested.

"No, no! Keep it on! I haven't

seen a woman—a lady—in an apron for years! Please keep it on! And do go on with the—the mess in the dish!"

"The mess"—she bent her brows reprovingly—"it's mayonnaise sauce. But I don't think—"

He jumped up to put the bowl in her lap. A sudden twinge in his knee wrung an involuntary groan from him. He walked a little stiffly toward her.

"You have rheumatism! And you sat all the time on that damp grass!" she cried reproachfully. "I thought at first it was the craziest thing to do, but I didn't dare say so."

He ignored the charge but smiled at the confession.

"And now you're not afraid?"

She blushed again. It was very becoming.

"It seems—it seems foolish to act like strangers when it's been so long—we remember so well—" She sighed a little. He studied her face—so like her sister's and so utterly different. The same gray eyes, but calm and drooped; the same clear white skin, but a fuller, yes, a more matronly face, a riper, sweeter, more restful curve. The soft dark shadows that accentuated Mrs. Dudley's eyes were lacking; a group of tiny wrinkles at the corners gave her instead a pleasant, humorous regard that her sister's literal directness missed utterly.

Nervous under his scrutiny, she rose hastily, and before he could prevent her she had brought him a roomy arm-chair from the house.

"At our age there's no use in running risks," she said simply, "you ought not to sit on the grass; leave that for the young folks."

Again he winced, but dropped with relief into the chair.

"Oh, one must keep up with the procession, you know!" he said lightly.

She made no reply; and as she lifted the bottle and began to beat the yellow mass again, it occurred to him that the remark was exceptionally silly.

"Does it have to go in slowly like that—the whole bottleful?" he inquired lazily.

She nodded. "Or it curdles," she explained. "The cook sprained his wrist yesterday. He never allows anybody to make the mayonnaise—he can't trust them—and I was glad to do it for him. He says mine is as good as his. Did you ever see him?"

"Well, no," Varian returned. "But he doesn't need to be seen to be appreciated."

A strange suspicion crept over him.

"Do you often— Do you do much— How is it that you—" He could not say it properly. Was it possible that Mrs. Dud— It was unworthy of her!

She caught his meaning, and her cool gray eyes met his with their uncompromising directness. He seemed convicted of unnecessary shuffling.

"Oh, Lizzie asked me not to do any-thing," she said quietly. "She wanted me to enjoy myself with her friends. But I'm not used to so much society, and I don't want to be any hinderance. I'm not so young as I used to be. I'd have liked the gayety well enough when I was a girl, but I guess it tires me a little now. There seems to be so much going on all the time. Lizzie says she's resting, but it wouldn't rest me. Do you find it so?"

He recalled his yesterday's programme: driving a pulling team all the morning; carrying Mrs. Dud's heavy bag over the links all the afternoon — she preferred her friends to caddies; prompting for the dramatics rehearsal, with a poor light, all the evening, while the actors gossiped and squabbled and flirted contentedly.

"It is not always restful," he admitted.

"It makes my head ache," she remarked placidly. "I like to see the girls enjoy themselves. I'm glad they're

happy — some of those visiting Lizzie
are so pretty ! — but I'm glad I haven't
got to run about so much. I'm very
fond of driving myself, if I have a good
quiet horse that won't shy and doesn't go
fast, and Lizzie has one for me — a white
one that's gentle — and I drive about in
the phaëton a great deal. The doctor
that came that night — were you here ?—
when Mrs. Page fainted and they couldn't
bring her to (it seems she was in the habit
of taking some medicine to make her
sleep, and it weakened her heart) asked
me if I wouldn't like to take out some
patients of his, and so I called for a very
nice lady — a Mrs. Williams ; you probably don't know her ?—and after that a
young girl with spinal trouble, and — and
several others. They seemed to enjoy
it, and I'm sure I did. Once I took a
young girl that's staying here — she had
a bad headache. She was a sweet girl,
and I liked her. She said the drive
helped her a great deal. It's astonish-

ing " — her eyes met his wonderingly — "how much trouble you can have, with all the money you want! I — I was sorry for her," she added, half to herself.

Before he thought he leaned forward, took her hand with the silver tablespoon in it, and kissed it gently. He admired her as he would admire some charming soft pastel hung in a cool white room.

"How sweet and good you are!" he said warmly; and then, to cover her deep embarrassment and his own sudden emotion, he continued quickly, "Are you very busy in the morning, always?"

"There are different things," she murmured, still looking at her spoon. "I have letters to write — I keep up with a good many old friends in Binghamville and Albany, where I lived with my married niece ten years, till they moved West. I loved her children; I half brought them up. One died; I can't seem to get over it —" Her eyes filled,

and she made no effort to cover two tears
that slipped over.

Varian took her hand again. " I know
about that — I know ! " he said softly.

" Then there are my flowers ; I do so
enjoy the beds and the greenhouses here,"
she went on more cheerfully. " The
gardeners are very kind to me — I think
they like to have me come in. Mr.
McFadden gives me a good many slips
and cuttings. I love flowers dearly.
Then I read a good deal, and there is
always some little thing to do for the
young girls here. They — the ones I
know — come in for a moment while I
mend something, or pin their things in
the back, and it's surprising how much
there is to do ! They fly about so they
can't stop to take care of their things.
They talk to me while I set them straight,
and it's very interesting. I tell Lizzie I
go out a great deal, just hearing about
their adventures, when she drops in to
see me. She never forgets me ; she brings

somebody to my sitting-room every day
or so that she thinks I'd enjoy meeting —
and I always do. She never makes a
mistake."

" Oh, she's wonderful," Varian agreed
easily. " There's nobody like Mrs. Dud,
of course."

She stopped her work a moment and
looked curiously at him.

" What do you mean by that ? " she
asked. " You all say it — in just that
way ; but I don't think I quite see what
you mean. Why is she wonderful ?
Because she looks so young ? "

" That, in the first place," Varian returned, with a smile, " but not only
that."

" Of course that is very strange," she
mused. " Now Lizzie is three years
older than I. You would never think it,
would you ? "

" No," he agreed, still smiling ; " but
then, Mrs. Dud looks younger than everybody. It is her specialty. I think what

we mean," he continued, "is her amazing capacity; she does so much, so ridiculously much, and so much better than other people. We try to keep up with things — your sister is a little bit ahead. She seems to have always been doing the very latest thing, you see. And all her responsibilities, her various affairs — it makes one's head swim! The women have set themselves a tremendous field to cover nowadays, and when one succeeds so admirably —" He paused.

She shook her head thoughtfully.

" But everything is done for her ! " she protested. " Why, I have never yet seen all the servants in this house ! And you know there is a housekeeper? Lizzie sees her a little while in the morning, that's all. And she never sews a stitch — there's a seamstress here all the time, you know, and that has nothing to do with the clothes that come home in boxes. And little Dudley has his tutor, and his old nurse that looks after his clothes.

What is it that she does to make it so wonderful?"

He only smiled at her perplexity, and she added confidentially:

"Lizzie wanted me to go to her dressmaker, but I didn't like the idea of a man, to begin with, and then I knew Miss Simms would feel so hurt. She lives in Albany, and she's made my dresses for so long that I thought, though she may not be so stylish, I'd better keep up with her; wouldn't you?"

A perfectly unreasonable tenderness surged through his heart. How sweet she was!

"If she made that dress, I certainly should!" he declared.

She smoothed the crisp lavender folds deprecatingly.

"Oh, this is only a cotton dress," she said. "But she made my gray silk, too, and Lizzie herself said it fitted beautifully."

She took up the bottle again: it was nearly empty.

"Now my mother," she began, "*she* was wonderful, if you like. Do you know what my mother used to do ? We lived on the farm, you know, like yours, and most of the work of that farm mother did. She did the cooking — for all the hired hands, too ; she made the butter, and took care of the hens ; she made the candles and the soap ; she made the carpets and all our clothes — my brothers', too ; and she put up preserves and jellies and cordials, and did the most beautiful embroidery ; I have some of mother's embroidered collars, and I can't do anything like them."

"It was tremendous," he said. "My Aunt Delia did that, too."

"We were old-fashioned, even for then," she said. "Everybody didn't do so much, of course, as we did. Lizzie says we were just on the edge of the new age. It certainly is different. And of course I wouldn't go back to it for anything. After we came back from boarding-school it was all changed. We moved, then, nearer the town. But, do you know, my mother went to singing-school, and Lizzie was looking that up in a book, the other day, to see what they did — she wanted it for a party!"

He laughed. "That *is* delicious!" he said.

"See what I found to-day!" she added, drawing a small object from her pocket. "I hunted it up to show Miss Porter to-night. She was so interested when I told her about it."

She showed him, with a tender amusement, a little slender white silk mitten. Around the wrist was embroidered in dark blue a legend in Old English script. He puzzled it out: *A Whig or no Husband!*

"That was mother's," she said, "the girls wore them then. She was quite a belle, mother was! And when people ask me how Lizzie does so much, I say that she inherits it. But at her age

[281]

mother was broken down and old. She had to be. There were nine of us, and here there's only little Dudley, and it was so long before he came."

They sat quietly. The setting sun flamed through the crab-apples and burnished the fur of the tortoise-shell cat. The mint smelled strong. The sweet, mellow summer evening was reflected in her handsome face, with its delicate lines, that only added a restful charm to forehead and cheek. He had no need to talk; it was very, very pleasant sitting there.

A maid came out to get the mayonnaise, and the spell was broken. He took out his watch.

"Just time to dress," he sighed. "Will you be here again? We must talk old times once more."

She smiled and seemed to assent, but her eyes were not on him; she was still in a revery. He walked softly away. She seemed hardly to notice him, and his last backward glance found the quiet of the picture unbroken; again it was a page from the Greenaway book.

He reached the terrace; laughter and applause from the piazza caught his ear. Fresh from the atmosphere he had left, he stared in amazement at the scene before him.

Swift figures were scudding from one to another of the four great elms that marked out a natural rectangle on the smooth side lawn.

"Puss! puss! Here, puss!" a high voice called, and a tall slender girl in a swish of lace and pink draperies rushed across one side of the square. A portly trousered figure essayed to gain the tree she had left, but a romping girl in white caught him easily, while Mrs. Dud, the tail of her gown thrown over her arm, skimmed triumphantly across to her partner's tree.

"One more, one more, colonel. You can't give up, now you're caught! One

more before we go in!" called the pink
girl.

"Here's Mr. Varian. Come and help
us out — the colonel's beaten!" added
Mrs. Dud.

"Here, puss! here, puss!" With
excited little shrieks and laughs they
dashed by, the colonel making ineffec-
tual grabs at their elusive skirts. Varian
shook his head good-naturedly.

"Too late, too late!" he called back,
and taking pity on the puffing, purple
colonel, he bore him off.

"Thank God! I'm just about winded!
I'd have dropped in my tracks," complained the rescued man, breathing hard
as they rounded the shrubbery. In the
corner two figures, half seen in the dark,
leaned toward each other an imperceptible moment. The colonel laughed
contentedly.

"When I see that sort of thing, I
think we've made a mistake — eh,
Varian?" he said, half serious. "It's

a poor job, getting old alone. Live at the club, visit here and there, make yourself agreeable to get asked again, nobody to care if you're sick, always play the other fellow's game—little monotonous after a while, eh?"

Varian nodded. "Right enough," he said.

"Different ending to their route!" suggested the colonel, jerking his elbow back toward the two in the shrubbery.

"That's it!" The answer was laconic, but the pictures that swept through his brain took on a precision and color that half frightened him.

He had no idea how frequently he dropped in at the little court behind the hedge after that. Sometimes he sat and mused alone there; more than once he took a surreptitious afternoon nap. He developed a dormant fancy for gardening, and walked with his new-old friend contentedly among the deserted garden paths. He studied her hair especially, wondering why it was that the little tender flecks of white attracted him so. At dinner he secretly tried to rouse in himself the same desire to stroke the gleaming silver fleece, high-dressed, puffed, and ornamented with jet, of the woman opposite him, whose hair, somewhat prematurely turned snowy, had won her a great vogue among her friends. But he never succeeded. She was absolutely too effective. She turned the simplest gathering to a fancy-dress ball, he decided.

He had supposed that it was the quaint privacy of their acquaintance that charmed him particularly — the feeling of an almost double existence; but when Mrs. Dud, who, he afterwards reflected, was of course omniscient, restrained herself no longer, and thanked him with a pretty sincerity for his delicate and appreciated courtesy, intimating charmingly that she realized the personal motive, a veil suddenly dropped. He gasped, shook himself, colored a little, and met her eye.

"I'm afraid I'm not so kind as you think," he said, a little awkwardly. "I've been an old fool, I see. Do you think—is that the way *she* looks at it?"

"Mary?" said Mrs. Dud, wonderingly. "Yes, I suppose so. Why?"

The naïve egotism of the answer only threw a softer light on the picture that had grown to fill his thoughts. He smiled inscrutably.

"Because in that case it is due to her to undeceive her," he said. "I am glad I have entertained her. I should like to have the opportunity to do so indefinitely. Do you think there's a chance for me?"

"What on earth do you mean?" asked his hostess, in unassumed stupefaction.

"I mean, do you think she would marry me?" Varian brought out plumply. "Is there — was there ever anybody else?"

For one instant Mrs. Dud lost her poise; in her eyes he almost saw more than she meant; the sheer, flat blow of it levelled her for a breath to the plane of other and ordinary women. But even as he thought it, it was gone. She put out her hand; she smiled; she shook her finger at him.

"I think, my friend, she would be a fool not to marry you," she answered him, clear-eyed; "and there was never," her tone was too sweet, he thought, to carry but one meaning—pleasure for him, "there was never anybody else!"

Varian walked straight to the garden. She was training a fiery wall of nasturtiums with firm white fingers. It occurred to him that he was ready to give up the tally-ho, and the Berkshires, and the scramble of pretty girls for the place beside him, to sit quietly and watch her among her flowers.

"I'm getting old—old!" he said to himself, but he said it with a smile.

For he knew that no boy's heart ever beat more swiftly, no boy's tongue ever sought more excitedly to find the right words. But when he faced her a little doubt chilled him: she was so calm and complete, in her sunny, busy, balanced life, that he feared to disturb that sweet placidity. With an undercurrent of fear, a sudden realization that he had no more the blessed egotism of youth to drive him on, he walked beside her, outwardly content, at heart a little solitary. At some light question he turned and faced her.

"You could not have all the greenhouses, but there could be plenty of flowers," he said pleadingly.

"Flowers? Where?" she asked.

"Wherever we lived," he answered. "And oh, Mary, I think we could be happy together! Don't say no!" as she shrank a little. "Don't, Mary, for heaven's sake! I care too much — I care terribly. I am too old a man to

care so much and — lose. . . . There,
there, my dear girl, never mind.   I
can bear it, of course. Only I didn't
know I'd planned it all out so, and—
But never mind.   I was going to have a
bay-window full of — "

He turned away from her for a moment.   But her hand was on his arm.

"We can plan it out together," she
said.

He knew how she would blush ; he
had even dared to think how directly her
clear gray eyes would meet his—her shyness was never hesitation—but he had
not dreamed how soft her hair could be.